ALEX WA

Death
of a Snoop

Penny Küfer investigates

Cover design: Estella Vukovic
Editor: T Shand

www.alexwagner.at

1

"Penny Küfer!" the instructor's voice thundered through the room. "With you, the safest place is in front of the gun! You can hit just about anything but the target!" The tall, extremely skinny woman shook her head and gave Penny a punishing look. "I have seldom come across such an untalented shooter as you."

What a bitch, Penny thought. This Ms. Steininger had the charm and teaching skills of a block of granite. She hadn't given a first name, but surely it was Brunhilde or something harsh like that.

Penny felt the stares of the other students on her and wanted to sink into the ground.

"Of your last five shots, no less than four haven't even hit the target circle," Ms. Steininger continued to nag. "And you should also—for heaven's sake, what are you doing! Are you trying to kill us? You're supposed to point the gun *forward!*"

Penny had turned to face the instructor, and her hand holding the revolver had followed the rest of her body. Which meant that the barrel of the gun was now pointed straight at the other students.

The instructor, however, had the reflexes of a panther.

3

Within a split second, she grabbed Penny's wrist and pushed her hand and gun back toward the target.

"Aim forward!" she repeated in a tone that went right to the marrow of your bones.

Penny put the revolver down in front of her and took a deep breath. The air in the shooting cellar, which lay deep underground, smelled all burnt.

Don't get rattled, she told herself. But that was easier said than done.

She wrapped a strand of her long red hair around her finger. A habit she had long wanted to break—only little girls fiddled with their hair when they were nervous.

The instructor was right, her previous attempts with the weapon had been miserable. But did Steininger have to tell her that in such drastic terms? In front of the whole group?

Penny couldn't stand being scolded, had hated it since she'd been a small child.

All right, if she was honest with herself, she had perhaps provoked scolding and other punitive measures more often than other children. *Far more often*. Being a good girl had never been her thing.

But she wanted to learn how to handle guns. She had to learn it, because today's course was a necessary prerequisite for acquiring her firearms license, which in turn was an important supplement to her fifteen-week training as a professional detective.

She was now about halfway through the program, and giving up was out of the question. Becoming a detective was Penny's dream—for which she had sacrificed everything. Her fiancé had turned his back on her when she enrolled in the Vienna *Argus Academy for Security Professionals*. He deemed such a career unworthy of his future wife, or some such nonsense. But he had been a terrible snob anyway. No loss.

Penny's mother, on the other hand, had unceremoniously disinherited her, which had been far more painful. Frederike Küfer was one of the wealthiest women in the country, and she too found her daughter's choice of profession highly unsuitable.

Penny had never gotten along particularly well with her mother, but she had to admit to herself that she had thoroughly enjoyed spending Frederike's money in a hundred creative ways.

Well, that was over now. Now it was time to complete the course, find a job as a detective assistant to gain the necessary professional experience and earn a living. Then, in a few years, she would start her own detective agency.

Those were Penny's plans, and nothing was going to stop her. Especially not some stupid little revolver that kept missing its target.

"You need to focus, Ms. Küfer!" the instructor's cutting voice brought her back to the present. "We're not playing games here; your revolver is loaded—with live ammunition."

"I know that," Penny grumbled.

"Right, then. Let's do another five shots, go, go! Don't dawdle around. And this time *into* the target, if you please!"

Firing a gun was very different from what she had seen on TV. It was loud—even though you wore sound-insulating ear protectors at the shooting range. When you pulled the trigger, you felt like the gun was going to explode in your hands, the recoil was so intense. Penny's arms were hurting now, even though she had only fired a couple of rounds. Not to mention the acrid stench of the gunpowder.

She reached for the revolver again, held it with both hands, and still didn't manage to pull the trigger. It put up so much resistance. She first had to cock the hammer on the back of the gun before she could pull the trigger. How pathetic!

In the days before the shooting training, she had already flirted with a stunning gold-plated revolver in mini format, which she had discovered in the store of the Argus Academy. The heroine of one of her favorite detective series owned one of those thingies. And this detective had no problem firing the gun one-handed! Never mind if she was crawling through rough terrain or chasing a particularly sinister villain. And, of course, she never missed her target.

Other than that, the instructor was wrong. Penny was not unfocused. She paid very close attention, just maybe to the wrong target. The student who was practicing with a rifle in the next lane had been distracting her.

Her name was Miriam, Penny had already learned that much during the last break—and something was wrong with her. She didn't shoot quite as badly as Penny, but she seemed so dogged about it. And so scared at the same time. She was completely out of place here in this shooting gallery.

Miriam's fingernails were chewed off. Her hands were shaking, again now, when Penny looked over at her one more time instead of finally pulling the trigger herself. She wore a silver bracelet with colored glass stones and decorative beads that looked like pink bubble gum balls. In between, small pendants dangled from the chain. Dolphins, owls, a teddy bear, even a wizard's hat. It was the bracelet of a teenager. Miriam, however, must have been around twenty-five. A few years younger than Penny herself. No longer a small child.

"Open fire, Ms. Küfer!" thundered the instructor behind her. Penny fired—and this time the bullet at least tore a hole in the edge of the target.

Yes! It was all just a matter of practice. *So much for being an untalented shooter.* Penny turned her head to her trainer—careful this time to keep her gun hand pointed forward.

"Go on," Ms. Steininger ordered, instead of finally giving her some praise.

What a bitter bitch! I bet she has no sex and doesn't eat enough chocolate!

Penny put took aim, but again Miriam drew her attention. The young woman's hand, which fumbled on the trigger of a rifle, trembled so much that the charms on the silver bracelet banged against each other like little bells.

Miriam also wore a dress that would have fitted in well at Sunday mass, but not at a shooting range. It was made of thick gray wool fabric, conservative and unimaginative.

When she had asked Miriam, why she was taking the weapons course—which any citizen of legal age was allowed to do, also outside of detective training—Penny had not received a proper answer. Just some rather vague excuses.

Miriam was the junior manager of a hotel in Lower Austria that had been in her family for generations. At least that much Penny had been able to find out.

That really didn't sound like a hot spot where you had to fear for your life. So why did Miriam need a gun license?

It was obvious with the other course participants. The group of nine consisted of two men who were taking the detective course together with Penny, two others who were training to be bodyguards, and a few nerds, angry citizens, and guys who could be seen to be gun nuts from a hundred yards away.

Miriam just didn't fit this group at all.

When Ms. Steininger finally let them have their lunch break, Penny tried to satisfy her curiosity. Otherwise, there would be no focused shooting.

She stepped up next to Miriam at the modest lunch buffet in the Argus Academy foyer, where Coke, coffee, and some munchies were available, and addressed her. "How's it going with the rifle?" she began. "Is it even harder to handle than the revolver?"

Miriam shrugged. She was pale, her blond hair could have used a new cut, and her rather large eyes looked uncertainly at Penny.

"Hard to say," she mumbled, then looked for a moment as if she wanted to add something, but remained silent.

"That's a fancy bracelet you've got there." Penny tried a slightly different approach. She pointed to the silver little-girl jewelry on Miriam's wrist and gave her a smile. Maybe getting a little personal would help to break the ice.

Miriam burst into tears without the slightest warning.

What the hell? Had she said something wrong?

Penny dug a handkerchief out of her jeans and handed it to Miriam. "Sorry," she said, although she didn't have the slightest idea what she was apologizing for.

She gently grabbed the blubbering young woman by the arm and led her out of the foyer, into a small backyard. A bit of fresh, cold winter air would certainly do her good.

Miriam dabbed at her eyes with the handkerchief, but her tears wouldn't stop flowing. "The bracelet is a gift from my grandma." She sniffled and stroked her fingertips over the kitschy, colorful piece of jewelry.

"OK?" Penny said. She wasn't quite sure why it was necessary to burst into tears over this.

"Grandmother is dead!" Miriam cried the next instant. She bit her lip and crumpled the handkerchief in her fist. "She was murdered!"

2

"Murdered?" Penny echoed. She must have misheard.

Miriam raised her head and jutted her chin. "Yes! Week before last."

With the sleeve of her dress, she wiped the last tears from the corners of her eyes. "The police claim it was an accident, of course. But it wasn't. That's why I'm here. I'm scared. I have to learn to defend myself."

She looked grim and determined, but at the same time her hands were still shaking like aspen leaves.

"I wish I could be like you, Penny. You're so fearless. And you handle those horrible things so effortlessly."

"What kind of things?"

"Well, the guns."

Penny laughed. "Effortless? I can't even hit the target!"

"But you're not afraid! I noticed that this morning. You're not intimidated by that old scarecrow."

"Ms. Steininger?"

Miriam nodded. "I think she's creepy."

"You're right about that," Penny agreed.

"And why do you want to acquire the gun license?" continued Miriam. Her tears had dried up now, and she didn't seem as closed off any longer as she had in the morning.

"I'm training to be a professional detective," Penny explained with a touch of pride.

"Wow. Really?" Miriam's eyes lit up.

Penny nodded. "Yes, and I've even solved a real murder case already."

She bit her tongue. She hadn't meant to say that. It sounded boastful, even if it was true. Her mother was a terrible show-off, and Penny certainly didn't want to become like Frederike Küfer.

But she was a little proud of herself that she had been able to solve the murders on the Occident Express. She had had to deal with a particularly insidious killer on the luxury train, but had been able to unmask them in the end. That was only a few weeks ago.

Miriam's eyes widened even more. "For real?"

"M-hmm," Penny said, then quickly changed the subject. "What makes you think your grandmother's death wasn't an accident?"

Miriam's lower lip quivered, but this time she kept control of herself. No more tears. She gave Penny a scrutinizing look, then apparently decided she could trust her. "Grandmother fell down the stairs," she said in a raspy voice. "At our hotel. But of course, she didn't fall, she was pushed! I'm sure of that."

"Did the police find any evidence of a fight then?"

"No. Nothing like that. That's why they insist it must have been an accident. But she *was* pushed. Which doesn't necessarily leave a mark on the victim, does it?"

Penny nodded hesitantly, but said nothing.

"I heard her scream," Miriam continued. "When she fell. And just thirty seconds later, I was at the stairs. My room is close by, next to Grandma's. I found her. She looked horrible. Like a doll with her limbs all twisted."

"How awful," Penny said.

Miriam swallowed. "There were footsteps. I definitely heard footsteps. Someone was running away. And that person must have been there when Grandma fell."

"And you didn't see who it was?"

"No, down at the foot of the stairs it was pitch black. Only at the top the night light was on. It was half past two in the morning. And from the hall you can disappear in all sorts of directions. The hotel is very spacious, even if most of it hasn't been used for a long time."

"And you think that this person you heard pushed your grandmother?"

"Yes. Otherwise, they wouldn't have run away, would they? I mean, if that someone wanted to walk down the stairs with Grandma, or was around for some completely innocent reason—they would have wanted to help her, right? When she fell. They would have wanted to check if she was still alive, and call an ambulance immediately instead of running away."

Penny agreed with her. Only someone who had a guilty conscience would abandon an old lady in such a situation.

"Grandmother was a detective," Miriam said, "just like you. Officially, she ran the hotel, but she was also an amateur sleuth. And a fantastic one at that! She used to solve murder cases. Brought criminals to justice. The police often didn't believe her, but she always proved them wrong in the end. And she was always on her guard, even if she got into danger more than once. Nothing ever happened to her. She was always smarter than the killers. It must have been a terribly cunning guy who managed to kill her. And that scares me—I mean, if Grandma didn't see through this person, how am I going to stand up to them? But I've got to solve this case, you know? I owe that to Grandma!"

She exhaled with a sigh, then brought the index finger of her left hand to her lips and began to nibble on the nail, which was already quite chewed off.

An amateur sleuth who used to solve murder cases? Penny couldn't believe her ears. She could have sworn that something like that existed only in books.

"What was your grandmother's name?" she inquired. "Should I have heard of her?"

"Johanna Lempra," Miriam replied, "but I'd be surprised if you'd heard of her. There have been one or two articles about her. But only in Lower Austrian local papers. In general, Grandma didn't like to draw attention to herself. She much preferred to work in secret."

"And was she just investigating a homicide when she ... was murdered?" asked Penny.

Miriam tilted her head. "Possibly. I think so. "

"You think? "

"Well, I've always stayed out of it, you know ... out of Grandma's snooping. I'm not like her. Or like you. It scares me – just the idea that so many crimes are committed that never even get discovered by the police. That so many murderers get away with their deeds. Or would get away with them if it weren't for people like my grandmother."

"I'm sure she was glad you stayed out of it," Penny said. "She certainly didn't want to put you in danger."

Miriam stepped sheepishly from one foot to the other. Then she wrapped her arms around herself. It was terribly cold in the small courtyard; after all, it was the middle of February.

Penny was freezing miserably, but she didn't want to interrupt Miriam now. Possibly her new acquaintance would shut herself up again when they returned to the foyer, where there was no privacy for such a conversation.

The story Miriam had just told her was unbelievable. But this young woman with the chewed fingernails didn't look like a notorious liar who made up fantastic stories just to be the center of attention.

"Actually, Grandma would have liked me to help her. She often tried to get me involved in her investigations. She even wanted me to follow in her footsteps, to continue her work, if –"

Miriam interrupted herself, swallowing hard. "Once she's gone. She was elderly, not so mobile anymore, you know? She sometimes asked me to help in her investigations. To stake something out, get some piece of info, do some research. Nothing dangerous. But coward that I am, I always shied away from that kind of stuff."

Again, Miriam began to bite her nails. But then she pressed her lips together and raised her head.

"Now I owe it to her, you see. I have to solve her murder. I can't just let her killer go unpunished. That's why I'm taking this course. So I can defend myself."

"Do you think you could fire a gun in real life?" asked Penny. "At a person, even if they threatened your life?"

Instead of an answer, Miriam looked away, seemingly embarrassed. "Yes, I do," she mumbled, but it was obvious that she didn't believe it herself.

"You said that your grandmother may just have been investigating a murder," Penny continued. "What did she tell you about this case?"

"That's just my problem," Miriam said, "Nothing at all. And that's unusual. Otherwise, she almost always let me in on her sleuthing, even when I didn't want to know about it. At least she always dropped a few hints."

"And nothing at all this time?"

"Not a single word. But I still think she was after something. Or after someone, rather. She was in that special mode. *Hunting* – that's what I used to call it. She always had this special look in her eyes when she was on the trail of a murderer. I can't explain it any better than that. She was spending hours pondering, musing, mulling things over."

Miriam shrugged her shoulders. "And for the last few weeks, she's been doing it again. But not a word about what she was working on."

"And you didn't ask either?"

"I was honestly glad of her silence. I thought she had finally given up trying to make a snoop out of me, too. That she had realized how futile it was. But now I think she wanted to keep me out of it because she thought this killer was particularly dangerous. And it must be someone from our midst. Someone who is staying with us!"

"At your hotel? A guest, you mean?"

"Yes. That is, not quite. We don't really run a hotel where guests come and go, you know. It used to be like that. The building is huge and has been in the family for a hundred and twenty years. In the days of the monarchy, it was a grand hotel that was very popular with summer guests. But nowadays tourism in our area is dead. It was already dead when my great-grandmother used to run the hotel. We have one or two permanent tenants who are staying with us and an occasional guest who wants to relax in solitude for a few weeks. A few hikers in the summertime. But that's it. Well, and some staff, because we also have a restaurant in the hotel. This is still running reasonably well, and we earn our living with it. We regularly get some customers from the surrounding area, because there are hardly any other restaurants left. Our whole district is a region where people are moving away from."

"What's the name of the town where your hotel is located?" asked Penny.

"Mönchswald. That's very close to the Semmering. The famous mountain resort. A little further south. A good hour from Vienna. Our hotel takes its name from the town, too. *Grandhotel Mönchswald*. We used to have five stars."

Penny shook her head. "Sorry, but I've never even heard of this town."

"No wonder," Miriam replied, "I was born and raised in Mönchswald, but to the rest of the world, my hometown is a lost place."

3

"A *lost place*?" Penny repeated.

"Yes. It sounds kind of romantic, doesn't it?" said Miriam, smiling shyly. "I got the term from Armin, one of our permanent residents. And he ought to know. He collects places like this. Abandoned and forgotten old buildings, churches, factories, sanatoriums, schools ... or even whole towns like Mönchswald. In our community there are more empty buildings than ones with inhabitants."

"He *collects* these places?"

Miriam nodded. "He writes books about lost places, shoots photo documentaries, gives lectures. He travels all over Europe and makes a good living, I think." There was undisguised admiration in her voice. "Armin thinks people enjoy the morbid charm of these places. The mysterious, sometimes even quite creepy atmosphere. As long as they don't have to live there."

"I see what you mean," Penny said. Places like the ones Miriam was describing had always held a strong attraction for her, too. "And why do you think your grandmother was killed by someone staying in the house?" She steered the conversation back to the murder case.

Miriam's brow furrowed, making her abruptly look a few years older. "It was 2:30 in the morning when Grandma fell down the stairs. By that time, our restaurant had long since closed. And no stranger was staying in the hotel. There wasn't a break-in or anything, either."

"So, you think you're living under the same roof with a murderer?" Penny said. What a terrifying idea.

Miriam nodded vigorously. "And there's something else. I haven't told anyone yet, and you must think I'm crazy—" She faltered and turned her head away.

"You can trust me," Penny said gently. "And if there's anything I can do to help—"

That was as far as she got.

"Would you really do that?" Miriam interrupted her. "Help me? Oh please, it would mean so much to me. I don't think I'll be able to do it alone. If I'm being honest. I can hardly sleep since Grandma died. And I can't eat either. I'm so sick with fear," she confessed.

"I'll be glad to help," Penny said, smiling encouragingly at her. "Tell me what I can do."

Miriam hesitated for a moment. "Would you … could you imagine spending a few days with us? At the weekend, perhaps? You could see everything for yourself; investigate, like Grandma always did. Surely you'll be able to find out who killed her!"

"You talking about this weekend?"

"Do you happen to be free?"

Penny had to admit to herself that she was in fact free—even if she didn't like it at all. Originally, she had planned a weekend trip to St. Anton am Arlberg, a chic winter sports resort in the Austrian Alps. Not because she was such an avid skier, but because she wanted to see Jürgen Moser again, the young police officer she had met during her murder investigations on the Occident Express. Quite some sparks had been flying between the handsome inspector and her, even though the events on the train had not exactly been conducive to romantic feelings.

But after that Jürgen had not been in touch. Not a word, not a phone call, not a text message. As a self-confident modern woman, Penny had finally taken the initiative and sent a message.

I'LL BE IN TYROL NEXT WEEKEND.
HOW ABOUT SOME COFFEE?

Casual chit-chat, completely noncommittal. Just don't give him the impression she wanted to see him again at any price. She had sent the text message on Monday. On Tuesday morning, Jürgen had replied.

HI, PENNY, GOOD TO HEAR FROM YOU.
I WOULD BE HAPPY TO HAVE COFFEE WITH YOU. I OFTEN THINK ABOUT YOU, I MUST CONFESS—BUT YOU SHOULD KNOW THAT I AM NO LONGER SINGLE. MY EX-GIRLFRIEND AND I WANT TO GIVE OUR RELATIONSHIP ANOTHER CHANCE. WE HAD BROKEN UP JUST BEFORE I MET YOU ON THE OCCIDENT EXPRESS. I'M SORRY ...

Jürgen had not mentioned a word about an ex when Penny had met him on the train. Which was probably because their getting to know each other had coincided with a murder case. But still.

Well, Penny comforted herself, now apparently a new case was waiting for her. So, it was a good thing that she didn't have anything planned for the weekend, and could check up on things at the Grandhotel Mönchswald. Who wanted to go on a date when there was a capital crime to be solved!

Miriam looked at Penny hopefully. "Do you think you can arrange to come to Mönchswald? I'll pay you a fee, too! I've saved some money from my tips at the restaurant. And there are hardly any opportunities for spending it at home."

"That's not necessary," Penny said. "And I'm not allowed to take a fee at all. It's not like I'm a professional detective by any means. I told you I'm still in the middle of my training."

Miriam shook her head. "I don't care about that. A gift, a donation, or whatever you want to call it, then. I'm sure you're a good detective. You've got that same look Grandma used to get when she went on another hunt. You've been eyeing me like her ever since I started telling you about the murder."

Penny said nothing in reply. Was it so obvious how much she loved murder cases? How much she longed to snoop around, ask questions, follow up leads?

It was her very great passion, no question, but still her conscience plagued her. Surely it was wrong to feel such enthusiasm for something as morbid as a violent death? Besides, she certainly didn't want to give Miriam any hope that she would actually be able to solve her grandmother's death.

"I'll try, OK?" she said to her new client, who at that moment looked at her like a helpless puppy. Big round eyes with nothing in them but a plea and unconditional trust.

Miriam nodded several times. "Oh, thank you, Penny! You'll get our best room and everything our kitchen and cellar have to offer! And of course, I'll help you as much as I can. I'll take on any handyman duties you give me."

"I don't need a sidekick," Penny said quickly. She was no Sherlock Holmes, who needed a Doctor Watson to unleash his full genius. She was nothing more than a rank beginner who had gotten lucky once. In her first murder case.

Her heart was pounding in her throat. Would the second investigation she had just allowed herself to be persuaded into be her undoing? Was she hopelessly overestimating herself?

If Miriam was right, and this killer had murdered an experienced investigator like Johanna Lempra, what chance was there for Penny Küfer, a student at Argus Academy who couldn't even hold a gun straight?

Or was Miriam deluding herself in the end because she couldn't cope with her grandmother's death? Had the old lady simply tripped on the stairs and died of natural causes? Had there really been a sinister figure at the scene of the crime, who had quietly stolen away instead of providing help? Or had Miriam imagined the footsteps in the darkness that she claimed to have heard?

The pain of losing a loved one could do strange things, especially on lonely winter nights and in a hotel that deserved to be called a lost place. In her detective training, Penny had learned a thing or two about the psychology of victims and perpetrators, although she had only skimmed the surface. There was plenty of reading on the subject waiting for her in her pile of unread books.

Might be a good idea to spend some time reading instead of sticking your nose into real murder cases, Penny told herself—but the next moment the fit of self-criticism was over. Real murder cases were just so much more exciting than any book could ever be.

"Penny?" asked Miriam. "Are you all right?"

"What? Yes, yes of course." She brushed aside her doubts and turned back to her newly acquired client. "You mentioned earlier that there was something else you wanted to tell me. Related to your grandmother's murder?"

Miriam hesitated. The hope that had just flickered up in her eyes gave way again to the expression of uncertainty and fear that Penny had been able to observe all morning.

"Are you religious, by any chance?" she asked.

Penny took a step back without intending to. "Err ... not so much, I'm afraid. Why?"

"Well, neither am I, actually," said Miriam, "but I don't think Grandma's soul is at rest. Or however you want to put it."

Penny looked at her uncomprehendingly.

"She ... has been seen. Several times." Miriam reached for Penny's arm, squeezed it tightly. "I think she's haunting the hotel! "

"A ghost, you mean?" *You can't possibly be serious.*

Miriam nodded fervently. "Yes. I know how that sounds. But I can't explain it any other way. And you do hear strange stories like that from time to time."

She squinted her eyes and brought one of her nails to her mouth again to nibble. "I think Grandma's trying to tell me that I must not rest. Not until her killer gets his just deserts. Oh God, I hope you can help me, Penny!"

4

Friday, February 8
Mönchswald

Penny parked her Jaguar sports coupe in the deserted parking lot behind the Grandhotel. Effortlessly, her little black kitten, as she affectionately called the car, had purred along the winding roads leading up to Mönchswald.

The place was located at almost a thousand meters above sea level and looked just as deserted and morbid as Penny had imagined from Miriam's description. Every other building in the small town was uninhabited or already in an advanced stage of decay. The most modern architecture to be seen here was from the Seventies. And on the short drive through the center of town, Penny had counted exactly two people on the street. Although it was just after 5:00 pm.

There were remnants of snow on the meadows and woods that surrounded the Grandhotel Mönchswald. Penny zipped her jacket up to the collar, then heaved her travel bag out of the trunk. As she closed it again, she tenderly stroked the black body of her dinky little sports car.

Soon it will be over. Soon she would have to get herself some old rust bucket or be buying bus tickets altogether.

The times when she had been living off her mother's money were over. Gone for good. And so were all the comforts that came with it. The Jaguar was no longer a luxury toy, but a cash reserve on wheels that she would probably have to liquidate soon.

Stop whining, she admonished herself. She wasn't a luxury doll crying over the loss of a car. She was a detective now! Well, unofficially for now—but she *had* been called to the scene of a murder. By a paying client!

She looked around. Tried to get an idea of the venerable old hotel that loomed before her in the darkness. It was more wide than high, consisting of a main building and two side wings, with countless turrets and oriels. Even though the ornate facade was in desperate need of a new coat of paint, the charm and elegance that this building must have once radiated was still visible.

At that moment, she noticed the man with the flashlight. He was just turning the back corner of one of the side wings, both of which were apparently completely unoccupied. In any case, there was no light on in either of them.

The man was walking slowly, no, he was creeping along—and seemed to be scrutinizing the windows on the ground floor in the feeble glow of his torch. Did the thing have weak batteries? Or had this guy, who was prowling around the house, deliberately turned the flashlight to the faintest setting? So as not to be seen?

A burglar? Here? He couldn't seriously think there was anything worth stealing in this godforsaken place.

Penny hesitated for a moment. The back entrance to

the hotel was directly in front of her, but it, too, was unlit. Was the house even still accessible from this side? Could she take refuge inside if this man was indeed up to something sinister? Should she confront him about what he was doing here?

She did not get to make a decision, because at that moment she was noticed.

"Hello, you there!" the man called, and then he came running toward her with big steps.

Penny froze in place. Getting to the back entrance now, before the man could reach her, was hopeless.

He lifted the torch, shone it in her face, and covered the last few meters that separated them remarkably quickly. Finally, he came to a halt in front of her, panting—and at second glance, didn't seem so dangerous.

He was quite a bit shorter than Penny and his shoulders were narrower than hers. On his head grew only a few hairs, which stood out wildly. This, together with his pointed nose, gave him a bird-like appearance. And his stamina wasn't the best either. He was puffing and exhaling steamy white clouds of breath.

He eyed her for a second in the glow of the flashlight, then scrutinized the Jaguar.

"Great car," he said, trying a whistle through his crooked teeth. "Don't tell me you're a guest?" He pointed a thumb at the hotel.

Penny cleared her throat. "You could say that. Yes. My name is Penny Küfer. And you are?"

He tucked the torch under his armpit and extended a gnarled hand to her. "Jakub. I'm the janitor. And the housemaid." He pursed his lips.

Hesitantly, Penny took his hand and shook it. "And what are you doing out here?" she asked suspiciously.

If the man was telling the truth and actually worked at the hotel, why was he skulking around the house in such a strange way?

"I'm providing security!" he said. "There's been an incident, and Miss Miriam has assigned me to look for clues out here."

"What kind of incident?"

He narrowed his eyes. "You're the detective, right? Miss Miriam mentioned your name. She said you'd arrive tonight, and I've already made up your room." Again, that pretentious tone. Apparently, Jakub saw himself in a weighty role in the old grand hotel.

But at least he seemed to know Miriam and also to have been informed of Penny's arrival. Which reduced the likelihood that he was a burglar after all. A very shrewd one, who might have spontaneously decided that Penny—and especially her car—was a more promising target for his efforts than the decrepit old building.

Without another word Jakub took the travel bag from her hand, then eyed her again.

"You're quite young to be a detective," he said. "And pretty." He twisted the corners of his mouth into a smile that was probably meant to appear charming. Which failed utterly.

"I didn't realize you had to be old and ugly to be a good detective," Penny returned with a grin. "But tell me now, what happened? The incident you mentioned?"

27

His smile faded, and for a moment he looked around suspiciously at the completely deserted parking lot, but then he finally spoke up. "There was a break-in, last night. Over on the other side, a basement window was smashed."

He pointed his finger at the side wing he had sneaked around earlier. "I'll take you inside, to Miss Miriam, then I'll check the west wing." Again, he sounded like a secret agent who served no one less than the Crown.

A break-in?

Penny followed the man into the hotel without another word. She remained on guard to see if he wouldn't try to bop her on the head with his twinkle of a flashlight and make off with her car keys.

But nothing of the sort happened. Jakub fished a huge bunch of keys out of his pocket and unlocked the back door of the grand hotel. Then he led Penny through dark, deserted corridors until they ended up in the hotel's foyer.

It was a very spacious hall, sparsely furnished now, but still impressive with its size, dusty crystal chandeliers and dark wall paneling. At the far end, a nostalgic old wooden staircase wound upwards—and on the steps of this staircase sat Miriam.

She looked distraught, no, almost panicked. When she caught sight of Penny, she jumped up and came running toward her.

"Oh, thank God, you're finally here!" She threw her arms around Penny's neck, almost smothering her.

A dark-haired man who had been sitting next to her on

the stairs appeared behind Miriam. He was the exact opposite of Jakub: tall, broad-shouldered—and damn good-looking. His chin line was hard and masculine, his body well trained, and even though he might be twenty years older than Miriam, he seemed very devoted to her.

More than just a friend, it went through Penny's mind. He put his arm around Miriam's shoulders as soon as she let go of Penny again.

"Armin Keyser," he introduced himself. "I'm a guest at the hotel."

"He's the lost places expert I told you about," Miriam added. "I'm so glad he's standing by me."

"That goes without saying," he said gallantly.

Miriam gave him an admiring look, but then her pale face darkened again. "Oh Penny, it's terrible. Someone's broken into Grandma's archive!"

Penny didn't answer right away, because something about Armin's outfit caught her attention. He was wearing expensive clothes, functional wear from a well-known outdoor label and light sneakers. Clearly not something you would have worn outside at this time of year, where it was freezing cold and muddy. And yet the shoes were dirty. Dusty, to be precise. As if he had been on a construction site.

Penny squinted her eyes. Maybe she should finally get the glasses the ophthalmologist had been recommending for years.

But yes, what was sticking to Armin's left trouser leg was clearly the remains of cobwebs.

Her gaze wandered upwards. And got stuck again

when she looked at his hands.

Armin's fingernails were perfectly trimmed, but there was some unsavory dirt underneath. His well-groomed hair, on the other hand, and his meticulously trimmed beard indicated a man who took personal hygiene quite seriously. Someone who cared about his appearance.

"Grandma's archive was burglarized." Miriam pulled her out of her musings. "I just discovered it earlier. They left quite a mess. Oh, Penny, I'm sure it was Grandma's killer!"

"Your janitor mentioned a basement window was smashed," Penny replied.

She glanced sideways at Jakub, who was standing next to them. He was still holding Penny's travel bag and apparently wasn't thinking about returning to other chores around the house.

He seemed to be downright enjoying the excitement surrounding the break-in. In any case, his dark eyes were shining, and he seemed to be following every word of their conversation closely.

"The basement window was just a ruse," said Miriam. "He wanted it to look like a break-in. He wanted us to think it was someone from outside."

Penny would have loved to know how Miriam had come to this conclusion. But the conversation with her client had to be conducted in private. Not in the presence of the janitor. Or this Armin guy, who was still holding Miriam in his arms.

If a murder had indeed been committed here at the Grandhotel Mönchswald, these two men were among the suspects. So, there was no question of discussing the case in their presence.

5

Penny put on what she hoped was a professional face and turned to the two men, "Gentlemen, thank you for standing by Miriam. I'd like to talk to my client in private now, please. I do think the situation is under control for the moment."

"Will finish my patrol," mumbled Jakub, who was clearly not pleased.

Armin, on the other hand, turned to Miriam. In his eyes was the look of a knight, gallant and concerned for the welfare of his lady. "Then I'll go eat something in the meantime, OK?" He gestured with his head to the other end of the hall, where a large sign next to a double door pointed to the hotel restaurant. "I haven't had a bite all day," he added. "But you know I'm here for you anytime, right? Call me if there's anything else I can do, no matter how late it is!"

Miriam nodded. "Come with me," she said to Penny. "I'll show you the archive."

The two women climbed the stairs side by side, but at the top of the landing Miriam stopped abruptly, bent over the banister, and called after Armin, "Could you let Willi know that I'll relieve him as soon as possible?"

"Yeah, sure," Armin returned, and then he was gone. Penny looked after him—and noticed out of the corner of her eye that Jakub, the janitor, was just leaving the hotel through the main entrance.

"Who's Willi?" she turned to Miriam, "someone else on staff?"

Miriam shook her head. "He's actually a guest. A permanent guest, that is. A childhood friend of my grandma's who's been staying with us since last year. He helps me out in the restaurant sometimes when things get busy, or I –" She faltered.

"Or you've just discovered a burglary?"

Miriam pressed her lips together and suddenly looked even more miserable. Penny was afraid she might burst into tears again. But she made a visible effort to pull herself together. She straightened her shoulders and held onto the elegantly curved stair railing.

"He's totally mothering me," she said, "Willi, I mean. Or should it be fathering? I guess he would have liked to have children of his own."

She sniffled, then suddenly a melancholy smile flitted across her face. "He's terribly clumsy at serving, but people still like him. I think it's because he always has an open ear, for everyone. Grandma wasn't much of a people person, even though she cared a lot about the hotel."

They went up another floor, then Miriam stopped again. A long corridor stretched out in front of them, insufficiently illuminated by two tiny ceiling lamps.

"Here we are," Miriam said. "Just to the right here that's my apartment. The first two doors. The next three belong to Grandma's rooms. The last one leads to her archive. There in the very back." She pointed down the hallway with an outstretched hand. "That's why I didn't notice the break-in until so late. I didn't check. It wasn't until just earlier, when I was trying to get into my apartment, that I noticed something was wrong with the door to the archive."

Her neck quivered as if she had to choke down a particularly bulky chunk. "The murderer must have broken in last night. I didn't get home until very late then."

Penny walked a few steps along the hallway, carefully stepping onto the wooden floorboards.

"How do you know it happened last night? Nothing creaky here. It's easy to sneak past your door when you're asleep."

"You can't," Miriam said, then gritted her teeth until her lips were just a bloodless thin line.

She raised her arm and pointed to a small plastic gadget sticking out of the wall above their heads. It bore a distant resemblance to a camera.

"A motion detector?" asked Penny in surprise.

Miriam nodded. "Theo installed it for me, right after Grandma died. I wouldn't have been able to sleep otherwise, all alone up here. I had to beg him to install the thing. But finally, he did it. When someone turns into the hallway here, a silent alarm goes off in my room. It's a very strong flashing light. It doesn't make any noise, but it still wakes the dead. So, I would definitely notice if someone came through here. That is, I would have noticed it if I had been home."

"And Theo is ...?"

"My fiancé," Miriam said. "He's a locksmith, works in Neunkirchen, the next bigger town. He lives there, too.

Only on weekends he sometimes sleeps at my place. He just went to his shop, to get some security locks. For Grandma's archive and for my own apartment. He seriously believes that someone broke in from the outside last night. Some gang of thieves, he thinks, who made it to our neighborhood. And he insists that Grandma actually just had an accident."

"I see. And no one lives here on the left side of the hallway?" asked Penny.

Miriam shook her head. "I used to. When my mother was still living with us. But she left when I was twelve. She married a Spaniard and moved to Barcelona. She couldn't stand it here anymore, she said."

"And you didn't move with her?"

"No. I like it here in Mönchswald. And I'm very fond of our hotel. I would never want to live in a big city."

"Your grandmother raised you then?"

"M-hmm."

"And where are the guest rooms located?"

"Below us, on the first floor. And in the past, of course, in the side wings. But they've both been shut down for a long time."

"And what's above our heads?"

"There's the attic. A huge collection of junk from the last hundred years. And the staff quarters. Only Jakub lives there now. He's originally from Poland, but he's been working here at the hotel for as long as I can remember. Irmi, our cook, lives with her family in town."

For a moment they stood facing each other in silence. Finally, Penny said, "So let's assume for a moment that the break-in at the archive happened last night. Was that the first time you hadn't been home since your grandmother passed away?"

"Yeah, right. I didn't feel like going out at all. But Theo really wanted to go to the movies." Miriam rolled her eyes. "After that, we went to a restaurant, for dinner, and I got home just after midnight."

"Together with Theo?"

"No. He stayed in Neunkirchen. He always has to get up very early in the morning. I drove back here alone. Oh God, Penny, just imagine if I'd come home a little earlier and possibly disturbed the killer. Whatever he was after in Grandma's archive."

"What did she keep in that room? Valuable stuff?"

"No. That is, for her, of course, it was vital. The archive was her data storage. For her detective work."

"A computer lab?"

"No. It's all old-fashioned. On paper. In notebooks. Best to see for yourself."

Penny followed Miriam further along the hallway. "Have you been able to determine what was stolen?" she asked when they reached the door of the archive.

"Only two candlesticks, I think. But they weren't valuable, a blind man could see that. There was definitely no break-in from the outside," Miriam repeated. "I'm telling you; it was Grandma's killer. The fact that he took the candlesticks was just for show. Just like the basement window being smashed. Look here!"

Miriam pointed to the completely battered door lock. It looked as if it had been worked on with a crowbar or something similar. The burglar must have really been undisturbed up here. Caused a lot of noise. And he was clearly not a professional lockpicker.

"Why would a stranger enter in the basement of the side wing?" asked Miriam. "Only to sneak through half the building and break down this one door of all things?"

"There are a few scratches on that lock over there, too," Penny said, pointing to the door to her right. "Your grandmother's apartment, you said?"

"Yes. But that was just done for show, too. He didn't really try to break that lock. You can tell. He just scratched at it half-heartedly to disguise where he really wanted to go. Grandma's archive. Grandma must have written something down about him. Or maybe found some evidence of a crime he committed. Maybe that's why she had to die and he came back now to destroy the evidence. What do you think?"

Considering that Miriam said she wasn't interested in detective work, she was giving the alleged crime quite a lot of thought. But maybe she was right. It seemed quite unlikely to Penny that any self-respecting burglar would have chosen the Grandhotel Mönchswald, of all places, as the target of his raid.

Miriam leaned her shoulder against the door of the archive and pushed it open. Penny followed her into the room—and stopped abruptly.

What she saw in front of her had nothing in common with what one commonly thought of as an archive. This was anything but a dusty data storage facility.

The room measured a good sixty square meters and

had an impressive stucco ceiling. The walls were lined with dark bookcases, all with glass doors. Penny stepped closer, peered through the glass, and looked at the books and magazines on the shelves.

It took her only a brief tour to realize that Johanna Lempra's archive was devoted to just one subject: crime.

Some of the shelves were stacked with crime novels - from cozy mysteries to the most violent thrillers. Johanna had also amassed an extensive collection of various true crime magazines. There were mags in German and English, as well as neatly stacked daily newspapers whose paper had already taken on a yellowish color.

A total of three bookcases housed specialized literature on topics such as criminalistics, interrogation techniques, forensics, and especially criminal psychology. There were also tomes on poisons and historical criminal cases, from famous to never heard of. Two particularly beautiful bookcases made of precious wood were filled with notebooks in all colors and shapes.

In the center of the room was a huge desk, also made of precious wood. Next to it were a sofa and matching fauteuils made of velvet with a floral pattern. The entire furniture looked as if it came from the founding era of the Grandhotel.

A few sofa cushions had been disarranged, a couple of glass doors stood open, and some books were scattered on the floor. Determining whether something had been stolen from this room seemed an impossibility.

Penny pointed to the two bookcases made of precious wood. "All those notebooks," she turned to Miriam, "are those your grandmother's case files? She must have been incredibly busy!"

Miriam screwed up her face. "Grandma was wholly dedicated to crime. That's how she liked to put it when she felt like joking around. Which wasn't often. She was frequently depressed—all the evil she exposed was getting to her. She didn't have a very high opinion of people, after all she'd been through."

"I can imagine," Penny said. Intrigued, she looked around. Only too gladly would she have delved into the case files of this late master sleuth right away.

"I get scared in here," Miriam said, reaching for Penny's hand. "It's always been like this. Yet I've only been here two or three times at the most, when Grandma was alive."

She shook her head. "I'm nothing like her."

"Why didn't you call the police, anyway?" asked Penny. "After you discovered the break-in earlier?"

Miriam let go of her hand. "The police?" she echoed, as if that were an entirely incomprehensible notion. "What good is that going to do? They won't believe me anyway. And I knew you'd arrive today. I knew you wouldn't let me down." She gave Penny a thin smile. "Besides, I'm sure Grandma wouldn't want a police officer to enter this room. She never talked about the existence of her archive in public."

"As an amateur detective, didn't she often collaborate with the police?"

Miriam snorted. "Collaborate? All they ever did was make fun of her. Yet more than once she helped them solve a case where they were completely in the dark. It was always the same. The officers took the credit, Grandma was downplayed to an insignificant witness at best. And they made fun of me just as much—when I told them I thought Grandma's death was murder. Not an accident."

"Who investigated her death, then? Someone from Major Crimes?" asked Penny.

"No, there were only two officers from Aspern. That's the nearest larger town. Apart from Neunkirchen. In the beginning, Grandma often turned to that station house when she had a suspicion. Or even concrete evidence of an undiscovered crime. But as I said, they didn't take her seriously, and at some point she just gave up."

Miriam walked over to the old plush sofa and curled up on it. "I called 112, of course, when I found Grandma," she continued. "She was lying so lifeless at the foot of the stairs, and I had just heard her scream. When she fell. Or rather, when she was pushed. I hoped so much that she had only lost consciousness, but her limbs were all terribly dislocated. That's when I realized she was dead." Miriam sniffled.

Penny settled down next to her on the sofa. Again, Miriam reached for her hand. "After the paramedics came the two Aspern police officers. And finally, the parish doctor. I told the policemen about the footsteps I had heard. That Grandma's killer was making off instead of helping her. They didn't comment on it, but they looked at me so strangely. In an old building like our hotel you hear all kinds of noises all the time, one of them claimed.

Especially at night. And the other said I was in shock because I had found my dead grandmother. It was a horrible sight, I admit. One I won't forget for the rest of my life. But I didn't imagine the footsteps. I certainly didn't. Then the two of them had a few short conversations with the other occupants of the hotel, whether they had heard or seen anything and so on."

"And did they?" asked Penny.

"Everyone claimed to have been fast asleep. No one wanted to have overheard anything. Of course, I asked everyone again afterwards. When the police had long since left. But they stuck to their statements. Absolutely nothing."

Penny considered. During her detective training at Argus Academy, she had learned about her limits as a detective. Under which circumstances she was under an obligation to call in the police. Her supervisor had spoken at length on this subject. Never mind that she hadn't even finished said training yet.

A smashed window and a broken lock were not among the cases where the police *had to be* called in. So, if Miriam didn't want to report the break-in, that was her business. And if Penny helped her—in a purely private capacity—to bring order back to chaos, she was not overstepping her authority.

Yes, that sounded quite good. Justifying things to herself that she wanted to do anyway—she had never had any difficulty with that.

6

"Why don't you tell me about the current residents of the hotel." She turned back to Miriam. "You mentioned that you guys don't run a very active business?"

"No," Miriam said, "not for a long time. Real tourists rarely stray into our neighborhood." She began biting her fingernails again. "That's what scares me so much. There are only a handful of people living in the house—and I know them all well. But still, one of them must have killed Grandma."

"Not a pretty thought," Penny agreed. "So, who do we have? Jakub, the janitor, who lives in the attic; Irmi the cook—she lives in town, you said. She must have a key to the hotel, though, right? "

"Yeah, sure."

"Your friend Theo got one, too?" inquired Penny.

Miriam looked at her in surprise. "Theo? Yes, sure, but you don't think –"

She broke off, seeming to lose herself in thought. Suddenly her eyes were full of fear.

"I don't think anything yet," Penny said quickly. "I just want to get an idea, OK? Let's start with the paying guests of the house."

"All right. There's Willi, Grandma's childhood friend and—"

"The one who mothers you and likes to help out at the

restaurant sometimes?"

"Yes. Wilhelm Lindner is his full name. He is a retired goldsmith. Worked all his life at a jeweler in Wiener Neustadt, but always commuted there. He had a great old villa here in town—or rather his wife did. The house belonged to her. She was pretty rich."

"Was? Has she passed way? "

Miriam hesitated for a moment. "Not yet," she then said, "but she's been living in a nursing home since last year. She has Alzheimer's, really bad. She doesn't even recognize Willi on good days. And they were married all their lives. Isn't that awful? Willi didn't want to live alone in the huge villa anymore, where everything reminded him of her, so he sold and rented a room with us."

Penny nodded. "OK, who else—the lost places guy? Armin, isn't it? "

A tiny smile flitted across Miriam's face at the mention of that name. "Yes. He's been with us since early January. Actually, his original booking was for a week only. He wanted to document the lost places in our area. But then he stayed on. The atmosphere of the hotel is just right for finishing the manuscript of his new book, he says. I think he'll stay with us until the end of March or so."

"And what does he live on? Doesn't he have a job to go to?"

Miriam hunched her shoulders. "I think he makes enough with his books and speaking tours. And as you can imagine, it's not expensive to stay with us. We offer good rates; every extra guest helps us cover the costs."

"Hmm, yes, OK. Let's move on then. Who else do we have?"

"That's all of them," Miriam said. She shrugged, as if she had to apologize to Penny for the hotel's abysmal occupancy rate. "Right now, business is slow even by our standards. We usually have a few more guests."

"Who's going to inherit all this, by the way?" asked Penny. "Your mother or yourself?"

"Me," Miriam said. "Mom wouldn't come back here for the life of her."

She seemed to ponder a thought for a moment, then continued, "As I said, the restaurant yields enough for us to survive. And in the summertime, we have a few hikers in the house now and then."

"OK," Penny said. "So, two paying residents in the hotel; Willi and Armin. And Jakub on staff. That's what I call a limited circle of suspects."

"But there was another guest, up until the time Grandma was murdered. A widow from Linz, quite wealthy, I think. Christiane Wittmann. She had been staying with us since the beginning of November last year. Her husband passed away, and she needed a change of scenery. She grew up around here, I think."

"And when exactly did she check out? Before your grandmother died? Or after?"

Miriam hesitated. Her brow furrowed. "I don't know exactly. Grandma always did the check-out. The bills and stuff. Anyway, the last time I saw Christiane was at breakfast. The morning before Grandma died."

"And that didn't strike you as suspicious?" asked

Penny, aghast. "That the woman disappeared the day your grandmother was murdered?"

Miriam bit her lower lip. "Now that you mention it. I guess I should have noticed. But if I'm honest, I completely forgot about Frau Wittmann in the days after Grandma died. Only just now, when you asked me about the guests in the house –"

She paused mid-sentence and ruffled her hair, destroying her last bit of coiffure. "I told you I was a lousy detective. I used to tell Grandma, too!"

"It's OK," Penny reassured her, "no problem. We're still at the very beginning, after all. I'm sure you have the woman's personal data on record. I'll take a closer look."

Miriam gave her a grateful but still pained smile. "Christiane didn't actually mention anything about leaving the hotel," she then said.

Penny raised her eyebrows, but refrained from commenting on how suspicious Mrs. Wittmann's behavior really seemed. And that Miriam should have been on the alert.

Miriam pulled her legs up onto the sofa and wrapped her arms around her knees. She nibbled on her lower lip as she did so.

"Is there anything else I should know?" Penny asked gently.

With a jerk, Miriam turned to her. "Did I tell you about the haunting? That Grandma has been seen, at night in the hotel?"

Penny nodded slowly. "You did. But that could have been just an, um, overactive imagination, right? Who's claiming to have seen her, anyway?"

"Jakub for one," Miriam said after some hesitation.

"And do you believe him? He made a somewhat over-zealous impression on me. Is he someone who likes to do a little snooping of his own? Poking his nose into matters that are none of his business?"

The corners of Miriam's mouth twisted into a wry smile. "You could say that, yes, I'm afraid. Besides, he's pretty superstitious. Every chance he gets, he kisses that angel locket he always wears around his neck."

"There you go," Penny said, "there's the explanation for the haunting. A superstitious janitor with a too lively fancy. Who else would seriously believe in a ghost?"

Miriam made no replay. She lowered her eyes and began to knead her fingers. Something was wrong with her.

Penny nudged her gently on the shoulder and gave her an encouraging smile. "Come on, out with it, you haven't told me everything yet, have you?"

"You'll think I'm crazy," Miriam said. "You'll be laughing at me!"

"I won't," Penny promised. "You're my client, remember? I'm here to solve your problem, however strange it may be. So, go ahead!"

Miriam still seemed undecided, but then she seemed to make up her mind. "I saw her too," she whispered, "with my own eyes."

"Who? Your dead grandmother?"

"Yes! I told you you'd think I was crazy –"

Penny raised her hand to stop Miriam. "I don't think

you're crazy. Tell me everything. What exactly did you see?"

"I was in my bed, asleep," Miriam began reluctantly. "And there she suddenly stood in front of me, in the middle of the room. It was dark ... but it was her, I'm sure of it. I could see her hair in the moonlight. Grandma had beautiful, almost waist-length white hair, you know," she added in a husky voice.

"And then? What did she do? Did she talk to you?"

"She said just one sentence, in a real scary voice, just like in a horror movie! *I am not dead.* Those were her words; I heard them very clearly. Then she disappeared again. Oh, Penny, I thought I was going to die of fright! I definitely wasn't dreaming; you have to believe me!"

"It's OK, I believe you. She just vanished into thin air?"

"Not exactly. She disappeared through the balcony door."

"And you didn't go after her?"

Miriam shook her head vigorously. "I was way too scared for that. It was really terrifying, I tell you! It wasn't until much later that I mustered the courage to get up and close the balcony door. By then it was freezing in the room."

"And you didn't see her then anymore? Out on the balcony?"

"No. Penny, please tell me I'm not crazy! I certainly didn't dream this. But ghosts don't exist, do they? Have you ever seen one?"

Penny shook her head. Then she began to ponder. *I am not dead.* What had the apparition wanted to convey with those words? That there was life after death? That Miriam's grandmother hadn't been murdered after all? And why did an alleged ghost need a balcony door to make his departure?

"Who issued your grandmother's death certificate?" she turned back to her client.

Miriam needed a moment to deliberate, then she said, "The parish doctor. Dr. Schopp. He has his practice in Aspern."

"And did your grandmother know him well? "

"Certainly. He was her family doctor, and not only that. There was also a love-hate relationship between the two of them, similar to the one between Grandma and the police. She would often visit his office on some pretext and then grill him about possible murder methods in one of her cases. She'd ask him about deadly poisons and things like that."

"And how was your grandmother buried?

Miriam shot Penny a surprised look. "Buried? She was cremated. At her own request. She's buried here in town, in the cemetery right next to the church. But what are you getting at?"

"I don't know yet. Was the mortician an acquaintance of your grandmother, too, by any chance? "

"Sorry? Here, everyone knows everyone. That's normal in such a small town. Grandma was even pretty good friends with Mr. Gergow, the mortician."

At that moment, the door of the archive was pushed open—and in trudged a red-haired young man in heavy winter boots. He had a toolbox tucked under his arm.

"'I'm back," he exclaimed, but when he caught sight of Penny, he fell silent, and the crooked smile he had just put on disappeared.

"This is Theo," Miriam introduced him. "Glad you're back already, honey."

Penny couldn't help feeling that this reunion lacked warmth—and the look Theo gave her in lieu of a greeting wasn't exactly friendly either.

Directly behind Miriam's friend Jakub, the janitor, scurried in. He was carrying Penny's travel bag, which she had left in the entrance hall earlier—but after a few steps he stopped and ungently dropped the bag. Curious, he looked around, then whistled through his teeth. Apparently, he had never seen Johanna Lempra's archive from the inside before and was quite impressed by the sight.

Theo pulled a baggy backpack off his shoulder and dug out the locks he had procured at his workplace. Then he opened his toolbox. Without further ado, he set to work on the door of the archive, and began to remove the old lock, which had been completely destroyed.

"I can only patch up the door panel for now," he informed Miriam, looking over his shoulder. "You'll need a carpenter, or preferably new doors right away."

Miriam just nodded. "You OK if I take over from Willi in the restaurant now?" she asked. "Or do you need me here?"

"Nope, I can manage on my own," grumbled Theo.

"Let's talk further tomorrow?" she turned to Penny. "Friday nights are always somewhat busier at our restaurant. It can get a little too much for Willi."

"I'll take Miss Küfer to her room," Jakub announced, puffing his chest up like a steward serving at a nobleman's castle.

Penny had to suppress a smile. "Mind if I look around the house a bit on my own?" she asked Miriam.

"Of course not," her client replied. Theo, on the other hand, didn't seem to like this idea at all. He gave Penny a suspicious, almost venomous look.

7

"If you'll follow me, please, Miss," Jakub said to Penny.

He grabbed her travel bag, trotted out of the archive, down the corridor, and then suddenly quite nimbly down the stairs. On the first floor of the hotel, he turned into the left of two corridors and finally came to a stop in front of guest room number 105.

"Here we are," he announced as he turned the old-fashioned brass key with tassel pendant that was stuck in the door lock. With a gallant gesture, he let Penny go first. "How long will you be staying with us?" He followed her into the room, put down her bag and eyed her curiously.

This man really had something of a bird about him, and it wasn't just because of his protruding hair and pointed nose. He was small, agile, and his gaze darted around the room, watching, as if his greatest fear in life was missing out on something interesting. Preferably something that wasn't his business at all.

"I'm going to stay for the weekend for now," Penny replied.

She looked around the room. Curtains of yolk-yellow brocade, which looked rather threadbare, billowed in front of the windows. A small crystal chandelier hung from the ceiling, but it too was long past its prime. The furniture in the room looked like solid wood, and it seemed to have withstood the ravages of time remarkably well. And the room was meticulously clean. Apparently, Jakub took his second job as the hotel's chambermaid very seriously.

Penny walked over to the balcony door and opened it a crack. Ice-cold air hit her, but she bravely stuck her nose out—only to close the door again immediately. During the day, there was certainly a great view of the valley from up here, but now only the lights of a small town were visible.

When she turned around again, Jakub was still standing in the same spot, blatantly eyeing her. Was he expecting a tip? Did he want to hear how much she liked the room?

While she was still thinking about it, the janitor already took the initiative: "A detective is the wrong person for our problem," he blurted out. "Don't take it personally, Miss Küfer."

"Oh, yeah?" was all Penny could think of to say. This criticism had come unexpectedly.

Jakub nodded eagerly. "Yes, definitely. Miss Miriam should have sent for a priest; I must have told her ten times. Begged her! Otherwise, the soul of Mrs. Lempra will not find peace, ever!"

Penny looked at the janitor, aghast. Apparently, *our problem*, as he had called it, was not primarily about bringing the hotel owner's murderer to justice.

A priest? To put her soul to rest?

It dawned on Penny what he was getting at. "You think Mrs. Lempra is *haunting* the hotel?" she asked. Jakub wouldn't be the first to make that claim, after all.

Again, he nodded. "I have seen her. With my own eyes. God as my witness!" He looked around the room and crossed himself—as if he expected a new materialization of his deceased boss at any moment.

Penny was overcome by a strange feeling of déjà vu. First Miriam had told her this ghost story, and now the janitor? Was this the result of living too long in a place as lonely and deserted as this old hotel? Did one become a bit whimsical over time?

"She was standing in front of me all of a sudden, in the middle of the night!" continued Jakub, unbidden. "Not fifteen meters away. And she actually asked me if I pushed her down the stairs! Can you imagine? After all the years I served her faithfully, she thinks I'm a murderer!"

He pulled a thin gold chain from under his sweater and fervently kissed the locket hanging from it—a golden angel.

"I am a God-fearing man," he emphasized and immediately crossed himself again.

"Where did you come across Mrs. Lempra's, um, ghost?" asked Penny.

"It was downstairs on the ground floor. In the foyer."

"And what were you doing there, in the middle of the night?"

The janitor's eyes narrowed to dark slits. "Checking if everything's in order here in the hotel," he said—as if it were only logical that one would sneak through the house at night for this purpose. He let the locket disappear back into the neckline of his sweater, then added,

"The walls in the house are thin, and I'm a light sleeper. Sometimes I wake up, and then I just stretch my legs a little. Do a patrol."

"You didn't happen to do one of those, um, patrols, too, the night when Ms. Lempra suffered the accident?" asked Penny.

For this blatant accusation, which was nothing more than a shot in the dark, she earned a bitter look.

"*That* night I was asleep," Jakub said, defiantly jutting his chin. Which made him look more like a bird than ever. Not a very threatening specimen, more like a disheveled little songbird.

Suddenly he raised his index finger and waved it in Penny's face. "You're barking up the wrong tree, missy! You'd better take a crack at this swankpot!"

"Who?"

"This Armin Keyser. He hangs around the hotel. At the most impossible times, I tell you!"

Now things got interesting. When people started accusing each other, you often got the most valuable intel. Even and especially about the one who made the accusations.

"Where did you see Mr. Keyser, then?" inquired Penny. "Not near Miriam's room, perhaps? "

"What are you trying to imply?" the little man burst out. "Miss Miriam is engaged to be married; surely you know that!"

Penny shrugged. "I'm just saying ... this Armin guy seems to like her a lot. And she likes him, too, maybe? There's nothing to it."

Miriam's love life was none of her business, but compared to Theo, the locksmith, Armin Keyser came across as a true hunk. Even if he seemed a little blasé.

Jakub snorted. "He was only going to stay for a week, that airhead," he griped. "And now he's been here for over a month. He's up to something, I tell you!"

With these words he turned and prepared to leave the room. But at the doorstep he stopped once again. Whirled around abruptly.

"By the way, that Theo isn't the right one for Miriam either!" he blurted out. "She deserves a good man, not some hothead! He's very rough with her sometimes, you know! That's no way for a gentleman to behave!"

He fell silent for a moment, seeming to ponder something. Then he asked, "What do you think of him? After all, you are also a woman."

Penny suppressed a grin. On the one hand, it was touching how the janitor cared for his young boss, to whom he seemed very devoted. On the other hand, he seemed to have a hard time accepting boundaries. The word *privacy* seemed to be completely missing from his vocabulary.

"I think Miriam will pick the right suitor," Penny said. "Without our help."

"Why, she's all alone in the world now that Mrs. Lempra is dead!" Jakub worked himself up. "She needs support!"

He turned to finally leave, but then something else seemed to occur to him. "Theo, that locksmith ... he quarreled with Mrs. Lempra the day she died. Before she was murdered! Maybe you should know that, since you're a detective!"

Even though Jakub had previously made it clear to her that she was only second choice for him—after a priest who was skilled at exorcising spirits—she now pricked up her ears.

"What kind of a fight?" she asked. "And how do you know about it?"

"As I said, the walls here in the house are very thin," the janitor replied. "Of course, it was not my intention to eavesdrop."

"Of course not," Penny said quickly.

She chose her following words carefully. "Could you possibly have overheard something anyway? Purely by chance? I'd love to know what they were arguing about."

Jakub shook his head, looking honestly saddened.

"No, unfortunately. But in the end, this locksmith left Mrs. Lempra's apartment, slamming the door behind him. Can you imagine that, such behavior?"

Penny did her best to look suitably shocked. Then the janitor finally took his leave.

8

Penny put the few belongings she had brought with her into the spacious closet of her room, then decided to devote herself to an initial exploration of the hotel.

She started with the hallway where her room was located, followed one staircase up, then another down, turned corners, crossed smaller halls—and soon had to admit to herself, not for the first time, that her sense of direction was lousy.

Soon she was walking through deserted corridors with threadbare carpets, past room doors that hung crookedly on their hinges; came across parlor rooms and lounges, found an old library and even a dance hall. The latter radiated something wonderfully nostalgic, but also a bit morbid—with its worm-eaten parquet flooring, the long since blinded mirrors and the crumbling stucco ceiling. Large parts of the former grand hotel had certainly not seen a guest in decades.

Penny clutched her cell phone and activated the flashlight function. Occasionally, dusty crystal chandeliers still lined the walls or ceilings, but the power was apparently only on in the occupied part of the house.

She felt quite queasy, if she was honest with herself. The further she went into the labyrinth of the old hotel, the more she had to admit one thing to herself: it was no wonder if you started seeing ghosts in this place.

She could not have told how much time had passed when she finally turned again into a corridor that seemed familiar. By nothing but a happy coincidence, she had returned to the inhabited part of the second floor—where Miriam and Johanna Lempra's apartments were located. And the old lady's archive.

Theo was kneeling in front of one of the doors, two rooms to the right of the archive, and was just stowing a screwdriver in his toolbox.

When he caught sight of Penny, he straightened up.

"Oh, it's you," he said. He wiped his palms on his pants, then looked at the door lock, which he must have just reinstalled. "Miriam can feel safe again now. No one will crack this one in a hurry." He pointed to his piece of work with an oily, shiny thumb. "Whereas the doors are the last trash. Nothing but plywood. They really need to be replaced, but of course we don't have the money."

Penny tried a smile and then wanted to continue on her way. Down to the first floor, to the hotel restaurant, where Miriam was surely still doing her serving duty.

But Theo stepped in her way. "Is your hair real?" he asked abruptly.

Penny stopped. "No, I'm wearing a wig," she returned with a big grin.

"I mean the color!" grumbled Theo. "The red."

Penny nodded wordlessly. "May I?" she said, gesturing to the locksmith to clear the path for her.

But he wouldn't dream of it.

"I don't like you putting any more ideas into Miriam's head," he began. "She's really scared enough already!

And I don't want my wife to own a gun. Or play detective like her grandmother. Women are curious enough by nature. They don't need to stick their noses in other people's business. "

"Yours is a distinctly modern worldview," Penny said, staring the broad-shouldered locksmith right in the face. If this hillbilly thought he could intimidate her, he was very much mistaken!

He shrugged. "I think everyone has their place in life, that's all."

"And where do you see Miriam's? Behind the stove with two children on her hips?"

Theo pursed his lips. "What's wrong with that? I want to have a family. And Miriam, too, someday, I'm sure. When peace and quiet return to our home. When some busybody from the big city doesn't make her believe she's missing out on something just because she lives in the country. Or tries to convince her that the world out there is a great adventure waiting for her of all people. Because that's not how life works!"

"You should know," Penny said. The guy getting on her nerves.

"Because the world out there can be pretty nasty," he continued, unperturbed. "We are doing quite well. Not here in Mönchswald, that backwater is dead, but in Neunkirchen. I have a good job there, and apartments are affordable. I will start my own business as soon as I have my master's certificate in my pocket. Then my wife won't have to be bothered by weird hotel guests."

"You're talking about Armin?" Penny demanded.

Theo pursed his lips contemptuously. "Isn't it obvious that he's after Miriam? That pompous guy! Trying to hit her up and talking loads of nonsense into her. *You've got to live your dream. The world is your oyster.*" He tried to imitate Armin's way of speaking, which was much more refined than his own. And failed spectacularly.

"It's a nice idea, isn't it, to have the world at your feet," Penny replied. "And there can't be anything wrong with living your dream, either. Can there?"

Why was she actually arguing with this guy? It was pointless from the start. She was here to solve a murder, not to be lectured by a hick.

She tried a frontal attack. "I heard you had an altercation with Johanna?" she began, looking Theo hard in the eye. "Right before she was murdered?"

Hothead or not, Theo was not provoked that easily. He just snorted contemptuously and screwed up his face. "Murdered? She fell down the stairs. She was old and not very steady on her feet."

"Oh, yeah?" countered Penny. "Maybe she was pushed, though? What were you guys fighting about?"

"A family matter. Nothing that's any of your business."

9

When Penny entered the hotel restaurant, a good dozen heads turned toward her. Strangers were apparently a small sensation here, and were to be gawked at extensively and without any scruples.

Even from the hatch that connected the guest room to the kitchen, a pair of eyes emerged and appraised Penny. A woman in middle years, slim, with short haircut. Probably Irmi, the cook. She eyed Penny with such undisguised curiosity that the young detective suddenly felt like an exotic animal in a zoo.

Miriam was juggling a tray of coffee cups between tables, her cheeks flushed. She didn't even seem to notice Penny.

Armin Keyser was leaning against the bar counter, his eyes fixed on the depths of a beer mug. On a stool to his left sat an older man with a thick shock of white hair and a similar looking beard. He, too, was eyeing Penny closely, but at least he was smiling at her. Suddenly he raised his hand and beckoned her over to him.

She hesitated for a moment, but then complied with his request and headed toward him.

"Wilhelm Lindner," he introduced himself after sliding down from his barstool and shaking her hand. "I'm staying at the hotel."

Johanna Lempra's childhood friend, Penny remembered. In front of him on the counter was a half-eaten plate of egg gnocchi, but now his curiosity seemed to have gotten the better of his appetite.

"You're the detective, aren't you?" he began, as soon as Penny had taken a seat on the barstool to his left. "Thank you for coming here to help us."

Now that was a friendly welcome—quite a relief after Miriam's uncouth fiancé.

"I'd love to," Penny said, "but I can't promise I'll actually be able to help."

"You're committed, that's the point," Wilhelm said in an almost solemn tone. "Allow me to take over your fee, whatever you have arranged with Miriam. I have some savings, while money is always tight here at the hotel."

A generous offer—which Penny didn't want to discuss further. First, she had to deliver results.

At that instant Miriam came over to them, gave Wilhelm a smile, and asked Penny what she wanted to order.

Penny opted for a Diet Coke and baked plaice with mayonnaise salad.

Miriam scurried behind the counter, grabbed a glass from the shelf, pulled a bottle from a drawer, and slid both across the counter in front of Penny. Then she stuck her head in the food pass-through and ordered the fish. Food service still worked the old-fashioned way here. Without computers or similar bells and whistles.

"You're the first one who seems to be pleased by my presence in the hotel," Penny said to Wilhelm Lindner when they were alone again. "Except for Miriam."

He took her hand and squeezed it gently. "Of course I'm glad you're here! If it helps Miriam to get some closure ..."

His brow furrowed. "She grew up in an atmosphere where crime was ubiquitous, you know. And she's not anything like her grandmother. Miriam gets all stressed out by murder, whereas Johanna ... Well, for her, capital crimes were the nectar of life, you could say. She loved the manhunt. And she had an almost uncanny flair for it. I can hardly remember a case where she was wrong. Can you imagine?"

Not really, it went through Penny's mind, but she preferred to keep the thought to herself. "Did Johanna talk to you occasionally about the cases she was working on?" she asked instead.

"All the time, yeah. We were close friends all our lives, you know." He blinked. Cleared his throat. He had probably been very fond of Johanna, there was no mistaking that.

Penny let her gaze wander around the room. People were eating, drinking, and having a good time at the tables. No one seemed to take any notice of her now, but that was just fine with her.

"Do you think Johanna was murdered?" she asked Wilhelm straightforwardly—and watched his reaction to these words very closely.

All she got was a shrug. "I don't know, honestly. I wish I had Johanna's nose for crime in just this one case. I guess murder can't be ruled out," he added. And then, after a short pause, "Miriam thinks it was someone from the hotel. One of the guests or someone from the staff. If that's true, we may all be in danger—and if not, please help her rid herself of that notion. So that she can feel safe in her own home again. It is so terrible how she suffers from this. And if there's anything I can do to support you in your work, Miss Küfer—anytime. Please don't hesitate!"

"Focusing on the occupants of the house for a moment," Penny said, "who would be your most likely suspect? Who do you think would be capable to commit murder? You know these people pretty well, I imagine."

Wilhelm hesitated. "I do, yes. I mean, I know them well. Jakub, Irmi ... and Theo. He spends a lot of time here, too. And Armin, of course, even though he hasn't been staying with us all that long."

"And what do you think of him? Could he have had any reason to murder Johanna?"

Wilhelm shook his head. "I can't imagine that. Of course he's lying when he says he's still at the hotel, just because he wants to write his book here, of all places."

He squinted over at the lost places researcher, who was still leaning against the counter but had since switched from beer to liquor. "If you ask me, it's about Miriam. She's the reason he's staying on. I think he fell in love with her."

Penny nodded, but did not interrupt Wilhelm's flow of speech.

"Frankly, I think he's a better man than that locksmith," he continued. "Even if he can't hold a candle to Miriam."

All at once, a tender smile played around the corners of his mouth. "I'm not her grandfather, of course, but I do care about her. It may seem sentimental to you, but I feel responsible for her now that her grandmother is gone. I want her to have a husband who loves her, appreciates her, and who will totally pamper her."

He was silent for a moment, his gaze lost in space.

"It's terrible to spend your life with the wrong partner," he then added. It sounded like an afterthought, something that didn't really concern Miriam.

Penny waited to see if he had more to say, but he remained silent. She gave him a moment to ponder his thoughts, then asked, "What about the hotel guest who left just before Johanna died? Christiane Wittmann. Did you know her well?"

Wilhelm looked undecided. "Hmm," he said, "not really. She was a very quiet woman, she hardly spoke to the rest of us, even though she had been staying at the hotel for months. She opened up to me the most, I guess I can say. Maybe she saw some common ground between the two of us. "

"In what way?" asked Penny.

Wilhelm rubbed his chin. His thick white beard rustled under his fingers. "She spoke a few times about her loss. Her husband, who recently passed away. My wife is still alive, but I have also lost her. She suffers from Alzheimer's, you know. In a very advanced stage."

At that moment, the door that led from the restaurant into the hotel lobby burst open. Theo came trotting in, stopped, looked around.

Miriam was cashing in at a table where a few older men were sitting. When her fiancé spotted her, he headed straight for her. He didn't wait for her to finish with the guests, but tapped her on the shoulder and then held a key ring under her nose. "All done," he announced. Then he leaned down to her and pressed a kiss on her cheek. "I've got to go, honey. Early shift tomorrow, you know. On a Saturday!" He groaned. "I'll see you tomorrow night. And don't do anything silly, OK?"

At the last words, his gaze wandered over to Armin and then to Penny in rapid succession.

Unbelievable. Such macho behavior! What on earth did Miriam see in this lummox?

Wilhelm seemed to be asking himself a similar question. When Penny turned back to him, his brow was furrowed, and his eyes rested on Miriam. There was unmistakable concern in his gaze.

"I never had children, you know," he began, "and that was a mistake. Family is the most important thing in life, don't you think, Miss Küfer? And love! I hope you yourself are in good hands in that regard?"

Penny's glass of Coke, from which she had just wanted to take a sip, almost slipped from her hands.

"Um, well," she stuttered, "I think there's room for improvement. "

She quickly changed the subject.

"How did Johanna Lempra actually come to be an amateur detective?" she asked. "You knew her when she was young, didn't you?"

Wilhelm nodded ... and smiled melancholically. "She

66

was a natural when it came to crime, I guess you'd have to say. Even as a teenager, she devoured every crime novel she could get her hands on—and was able to solve every case. Often within the first half of the book. I still remember how many evenings we spent together in front of the radio. Mystery radio dramas were a very popular entertainment back then, you know. But Johanna followed real murder investigations with even greater passion. At first in the newspaper, later also on television. And even then, she sometimes seemed like a clairvoyant. She usually knew the solution before the police did, and solved cases that others had long given up on. Unfortunately, the official authorities, especially our local police, were not really willing to acknowledge her genius until her death."

10

As Penny ate her fish, and the restaurant increasingly emptied, Wilhelm slid off his barstool.

"Excuse me," he mumbled, stepping into the path of Miriam, who was just coming out of the kitchen. "Call it a day. I'll take over here and lock up later. You'll want to take care of your guest." He gestured with his head toward Penny.

Miriam was only too happy to accept the offer. She tied off her serving apron and pressed a bunch of keys into Wilhelm's hand. The old man disappeared behind the bar and began to process the last drink orders.

"I'd love to take a closer look at your grandmother's archive," Penny said as she walked out of the restaurant at Miriam's side.

Miriam stopped abruptly, causing Penny to almost collide with her. "So, you also think that Grandma was killed because of her work? That there's a killer among us that she knew too much about?"

Penny raised both hands defensively. How were you supposed to make sure that your frightened client didn't attach a new hope to every word you said?

She put her hand on Miriam's shoulder. "You have to have a little patience, OK? There's no point in us speculating wildly. We have to gather the facts first, question the possible suspects ... do the legwork, you know? Only then does it make sense to draw conclusions. Agreed?"

Penny felt pretty awkward during this sermon. She was still a student at the detective academy and here she was making big speeches about professional investigative work?

What have you gotten yourself into again with this murder case? she asked herself silently—and not for the first time. Her thirst for adventure was occasionally greater than her common sense.

At this hour of the night, Johanna Lempra's archive was a gloomy and rather eerie place. The motley selection of wall and floor lamps provided only dim light. The old furniture and dark bookshelves cast long shadows. And the books on the shelves, which were about nothing but acts of blood, seemed to flock together, moving menacingly closer.

Don't be such a scaredy-cat, Penny tried to hearten herself. It's just a somewhat special library, nothing more.

She came to stand in front of the two bookcases that housed Johanna's notebooks.

"How did your grandmother keep her case files organized?" She turned to Miriam, who stayed close behind her. The eerie atmosphere of the archive seemed to affect her much more than it had Penny.

"I don't know," Miriam said, "I've always avoided this room." Her voice was little more than a whisper, though there was no need for secrecy at all. They were alone in here—if you disregarded the company of all the violent criminals whose stories were recorded in Johanna Lempra's books.

Johanna must have had a weakness for fine stationery. Her notebooks had the most beautiful covers. Diaries of a model student—with a passion for crime.

The volumes in the left of the two bookcases looked newer, less yellowed. The very bottom shelf was still empty—as if Johanna Lempra had divided the space for her case files according to her lifetime.

Penny opened the glass doors and began pulling notebooks at random from the shelves. She turned a few pages of each volume ... and came across pasted photos, newspaper clippings, and pages of reports in legible handwriting.

After a few minutes, she turned to Miriam, who stood motionless behind her.

"Your grandmother made it easy for us. She dated all her entries. Without exception. She actually kept a sort of diary of crime. Fascinating. And—hey, what's that?" Penny faltered.

The book she had just opened was missing a few pages. Quite a few pages, in fact—a few in the front and some further back, too. What did that mean?

She carried the book over to the desk and placed it there. "Who tears pages out of their case files? Even more so when they are such fine paper goods?"

"Grandma certainly didn't," Miriam replied.

"Hmm." Penny returned to the open bookcase and turned to the next shelf.

"Give me a hand, please," she said. "Check out the

books up there—see if anything's been ripped out of them, too."

Miriam nodded hesitantly. It seemed to cost her some effort to have to get so close to her grandmother's case files. Nevertheless, she did as she was told.

"Now, as I see it, pages are missing exclusively from notebooks of the last eight months," Penny summed up a scant half hour later. "Several volumes from that time period are affected, with no regular pattern that I can see. Did you find anything in the older books? Were any pages torn out of those, too?"

"Not as far as I can see." Miriam put one of the notebooks back on the shelf and once again began biting her fingernails.

"So that was the reason for the break-in," she said after a little while. She spoke again in a whisper and with an expression of utmost tension on her face. "Grandma must have written down something about the murderer in her notebooks!"

"Not so fast," said Penny. "Your grandmother might have torn out the pages herself. Which would be unusual, but who knows? Maybe she wanted to erase certain content that way? Something she got wrong, for example?"

Miriam shook her head vigorously. "Certainly not. Grandmother never even crossed anything out. Look here." She picked up a pen from the desk and held it out to Penny.

"An ink eraser? They still make those?" Suddenly,

memories of school days rose in Penny's mind.

Miriam nodded. "Grandma would never have torn pages out of a book or notebook. She always got terribly angry when I did that as a child. *Treat the written word with respect,* she always preached to me. And mistakes were there to be learned from. That's why you didn't try to erase the memory of them, but regarded them as teachers and cherished them. Even the ink eraser was only to be used for minor spelling mistakes. Not to change content afterwards. Grandma was really very particular about that."

"Hmm," said Penny. She reopened one of the note-books she had just looked through. Miriam was right. The writing was almost calligraphy; everything looked as if it had been drawn with a ruler. And not a single word had been crossed out anywhere.

Now and then Johanna had pasted something in, pho-tos, newspaper clippings and the like—but she had also taken extreme care in doing so. The conclusion that the old lady had not defaced her notebooks herself was therefore permissible. And since no one but Johanna had entered this archive during her lifetime, only the burglar of the previous night could be behind this van-dalism.

Penny grabbed the latest three notebooks, out of the five total that were missing pages. She handed the other two to Miriam.

"We need to read them. Find out if there's anything in here that can give us a clue to Johanna's killer. Although probably those very pages will be missing. But maybe we'll get lucky, and the burglar has overlooked something."

Miriam backed away as if Penny were holding a poisonous snake toward her. "I don't want to read them," she said, "I get nightmares from Grandma's cases."

"Hmm. Well then, I'll read them myself. Can you at least look through the desk? The drawers? Maybe there are some notes, evidence, whatever. Set aside whatever seems interesting or strange to you, OK? I'll take a closer look at it then."

Miriam nodded hesitantly. She would certainly have liked to avoid this more harmless task, too—but Penny didn't let her off the hook this time. It would take quite a while for the two of them to go through Johanna's archive, and any helper other than Miriam was out of the question. Not in a house where everyone was a murder suspect.

She retreated to the velvet sofa with the battered five notebooks and immersed herself in the old detective's reports. She read in chronological order, starting with the oldest notebook. Johanna had started it last summer.

Penny had always been interested in crime, just like Johanna, and had therefore devoured a wealth of crime literature in her lifetime. Novels as well as articles or books about true crimes.

However, she had never come across anything like Johanna Lempra's diaries. The old lady reported so meticulously that one had the feeling of being able to look over her shoulder during her investigations.

73

And yet there was often no indication of *how* the master sleuth had arrived at the right solution at the end of each case. Presumably, her own thought processes had been self-evident to her, as opaque as they might be to an outsider.

The oldest of the five books was devoted to a total of three cases. First, an insidious assassination attempt in the community of Aspern, which the police had dismissed as a common heart attack.

Second: a spectacular multiple murder case in Vienna, which Penny herself had followed in the newspapers, and which, as far as she knew, was still officially unsolved. Johanna named a man as the murderer who had certainly not been mentioned in the press.

And third: a poison murder in the Waldviertel, the northern part of Austria, apparently within a family with whom Johanna had been friends.

Several pages had been torn out after the first case, and a few more after the third.

Between her murder investigations, the old lady had also occasionally noted down private things. Thoughts about Miriam, the solution to a TV mystery she had already come up with in the first half of the movie, comments on current events, and the like.

The next three notebooks Penny looked at followed a similar pattern. They each contained several cases, with pages repeatedly missing between them. Apparently, whoever had torn out the sheets had gone through the books carefully, destroying everything that could have helped Penny in any way.

In the fifth book, most of the pages had been removed. More was missing than had been left intact. But Penny had barely flipped through the first few of the remaining pages when she came across a most interesting passage. The note followed a review of a television detective story that Penny herself had seen and found rather boring, and read as follows:

Armin can't fool me; he's not really interested in Miriam. I have to protect her from him.
Should I tell him outright that I know what he's really after in the hotel?

Penny looked up and over at Miriam, who was in the process of rummaging through the desk drawers. She was about to call her name to get her client's attention, but then changed her mind.

Let's first find out what Johanna Lempra was getting at with this cryptic remark.

Armin was decidedly a better friend to Miriam than that troll Theo, in Penny's opinion. He seemed genuinely fond of her. And Miriam seemed to like him, too.

Penny decided not to destroy those budding feelings with a grandmother's suspicions that might ultimately prove unfounded. Using her cell phone, she photographed the passage about Armin, then delved again into the last of Johanna's diaries. She turned page after page, and could feel fatigue pressing on her eyelids. But then she was suddenly wide awake.

Christiane Wittmann is a murderer, it said, in Johanna's

immaculate handwriting. Just a few pages after the cryptic note about Armin.

Penny had to read the entry twice. It was dated January 12, just two weeks before Johanna's death.

Christiane Wittmann, the quiet, grieving widow Wilhelm Lindner had described to her just before in the restaurant, was supposed to be a murderess?

Quickly, Penny read on. The entry for January 15 read:

I was not wrong about Christiane. I accused her outright of the murders, and she confessed to both crimes. Then, however, she made fun of me for not having a shred of evidence. Which, unfortunately, she is right about.
I don't know yet what poison she used. Both her husband and son-in-law died of natural causes according to the police. If I can find out, I may have a chance yet to prove her guilty.

Here the report ended. The next pages—the last ones in this notebook—had all been torn out. Penny sat back and groaned in frustration.

A chance yet to prove her guilty ...

Was that why Johanna had been murdered? Because in the end she had succeeded in finding evidence against a ruthless double murderer? Had the old master sleuth paid for this detective feat with her life?

Penny glanced over at Miriam—and was astonished to find her standing rooted to the spot in front of the desk. In her right hand, she held a pale blue sheet of stationery, on which her gaze was frozen. The matching envelope lay directly in front of her on the tabletop.

"What is it?" asked Penny in alarm. "Did you find something?"

Miriam lowered the paper and stared at her open-mouthed. "A letter from Grandma," she whispered, "to me."

"Oh." Penny tried not to let her disappointment show. She'd been hoping for something that could get her ahead. In the murder case.

"What is she trying to tell me?" asked Miriam—reading unbidden from the letter to Penny: "*Learn from the past, my beloved Miriam, and you will never be a beggar again.* I don't understand what that means."

"That makes two of us," Penny said. She stood up, walked over to Miriam, and peered over her shoulder. The letter was written in the same beautiful handwriting as the diaries.

... you will never be a beggar again. This wording was very strangely chosen. Of course, Johanna's grand-daughter was not exactly wealthy, but a beggar?

"Sounds to me like she's trying to promise you some-thing," Penny said to Miriam, "an inheritance, perhaps?"

Miriam furrowed her brow. "Yeah, sure, I'm her heiress. I get the hotel. But that's all. The notary has already opened Grandma's will. "

"Where did you find the letter?" asked Penny.

"Up here, in the first drawer on the left."

"And what else was in there?"

Miriam shrugged. "Insurance policies, tax returns. I guess it was Grandma's drawer for important documents."

"So, she placed the letter in a place where you would definitely find it," Penny reasoned aloud.

"Yes, but the words don't make sense, do they?"

"Can I take a picture of the letter? I'll think about it, OK? Maybe I'll come up with something—but first we want to find your grandma's killer, don't we?"

"Yeah ... sure," Miriam said quickly.

"I've come across a promising lead," Penny continued. "In your grandmother's last diary."

She gave Miriam a short summary of the *Christiane Wittmann* case. Two men dead, an unknown poison ... and for the time being no usable evidence that could have convicted the murderer.

When Penny had finished, her client had gone pale and was looking at her out of eyes wide with terror.

"Christiane? A murderess? But she was such a nice lady! Not very talkative, but still kind. Completely harmless!"

"Even nice people can be killers," Penny replied—then stood up and snapped a photo of the strange letter Johanna Lempra had left for her granddaughter.

11

Saturday, February 9

It was already after midnight when Penny dropped into her bed. The mattress was worn out, but the bed linen was spotless white and pleasantly scented.

When she was almost asleep, there was a knock at the door. She pulled herself up, put on her pajamas backwards—which she noticed too late, but didn't care much about at this hour.

Irmi, the cook, stood in front of the door with a food tray in her hands. With her short haircut and slim, no, almost athletic figure, she looked more like a fitness trainer than the typical cook of a country restaurant.

She smiled broadly when she caught sight of Penny. "You haven't been sleeping yet, have you?"

She stepped into the room without waiting for a replay. "You've eaten so little tonight, I thought I'd bring you another dessert."

Nice excuse, Penny thought. The portion of baked plaice she had eaten in the restaurant had been more than generous. The fact that Irmi now came to her after midnight with two large pieces of chocolate cake had absolutely nothing to do with Penny's physical well-being. The cook was simply curious—like the janitor before her. Apparently, this was a widespread trait at the

Grandhotel Mönchswald.

Well, Penny didn't mind. The cook was also on the list of possible suspects, so a conversation with her was inevitable anyway. Apart from that, the chocolate cake smelled so irresistible that Penny actually felt a pang of appetite.

No sooner had she settled down at the narrow desk in her room and speared the first piece of cake on her fork than Irmi began to talk.

"You're going to catch him, aren't you?" she asked excitedly. "The one who did this to Johanna. That dastardly assassin! And then, I hope, they will punish him severely! In Austria, we are far too lenient with scum like that."

Penny nodded with her mouth full. The cake tasted even more delicious than expected. "I'll try my best," she said.

"Right!" Irmi replied with fervor. "An eye for an eye, a tooth for a tooth, I say. That may be old-fashioned, but it's fair! There'd be a lot less murders, rapes or robberies if these bastards were punished more severely, I give you my word on that!"

Penny had been right; the cook wanted to talk about the murder. Just like the janitor had done before. Well, that was a good thing, even if Penny's little gray cells were already half asleep.

She seized the opportunity and got straight to the point. "Mrs. Lempra's killer must be someone from the hotel, right?"

The cook nodded. "Yes, that's what it looks like. Isn't it

awful!" Her voice sounded more excited than frightened.

"Quite awful," Penny confirmed. "So, who do you think would be the most likely culprit?"

Irmi didn't have to think about it first. "I don't know. I wouldn't put murder past anyone here. Evil is everywhere!"

"Anyone? Miriam too? "

The cook hesitated.

"You can't be fooled by an innocent exterior," she then said. "There is something evil in so many humans. Even in people you'd never think capable of it. Johanna really opened my eyes to that!" She rubbed her hands together, almost as if this experience had given her great pleasure.

"It seems to me that you are also quite a passionate amateur sleuth, Irmi. Just like your late boss?"

The cook visibly enjoyed the compliment, but lowered her eyes in a touch of modesty. "I have learned a lot from Mrs. Lempra. All of us here in the hotel. Even if some have appreciated it less. But I would never compare my talents to hers."

"Did she discuss her cases with you, then?"

"Yes, quite often. With all of us. Well, except with Miriam; she's so squeamish. Prefers to deny evil rather than face it. And Johanna was discreet in front of the guests, of course. She confided in me and Jakub and of course in Mr. Lindner. She always said that talking through her cases with someone helped her get her thoughts in order. Going through different possibilities. Sometimes being able to take a different angle."

Irmi perched unbidden on the single armchair that

stood beside Penny's bed. "None of us let anything leak to the outside world," she continued. "That's where we maintained a strict code of honor. Johanna wasn't exactly popular in the community, I'm sorry to say. Her abilities were scary to people. And more of your neighbors than you might imagine in your worst nightmares probably have a skeleton in their closet."

"Have you ever been able to help Mrs. Lempra solve a case?" asked Penny.

The cook tilted her head. "Well, I was able to make a small contribution once or twice, perhaps. Anyway, I've always tried very hard."

"And Mr. Lindner?"

"Oh, he could have listened to Johanna for hours. He's very devoted to her, you know. That is, he was very devoted to her."

For a moment, the euphoric sparkle disappeared from Irmi's eyes and gave way to an expression Penny couldn't interpret. Was it sorrow? Or something else?

"What about Jakub?" she asked further.

"Oh, that's a real wannabe snoop. He's totally overestimating himself, if you ask me."

"But overall, you've all learned a few things as far as violent crime is concerned."

The cook's eyes narrowed. "What are you trying to say?"

"Just that maybe the killer knew what he was doing if we actually have to look for the culprit among the occupants of this house."

Irmi snorted. "You can leave me out of it, Miss! I didn't

kill Johanna. I am a peace-loving woman! I hope you have that much knowledge of human nature."

She shot Penny a punishing glance, then continued: "You'd better take a look at this Armin Keyser. He's a bad one, I tell you! Wouldn't surprise me if he's our killer." She hesitated.

"Yes? Why?" Penny inquired. "What motive could he have had for murdering Johanna?" She put down the cake fork. If she ate another bite, she would burst.

But things went well with Irmi, after all. She was not only an excellent cook, but also a very fertile chatterbox.

Gossip is a professional detective's best friend, one of Penny's instructors at the Argus Academy used to say. He was undoubtedly right.

Irmi raised an index finger. "He's a treasure hunter, this Armin! He has really been pestering my great-aunt Leonora ... about that old matter."

"A treasure hunter?" Penny repeated. She frowned. Was the cook pulling her leg?

Irmi nodded triumphantly. "Yep. But of course he's barking up the wrong tree." She made a snide hand gesture. "Leonora's got him fooled. She's spouting complete nonsense, trying to give herself airs ... and she's getting senile, too, I'm afraid. "

Still, Irmi didn't miss the opportunity to give Penny a full report of the "nonsense" her great-aunt had apparently related to Armin. "It's about Johanna's grandfather," she said. "Matthias ... I can't remember the family name. He ran the hotel during the war years. And they say he was a Nazi sympathizer. Although he hid a Jewish

83

couple here in the hotel. Don't you like the cake? You've hardly eaten half of it!"

"Oh yes, it's delicious," Penny said quickly, reaching guiltily for her fork. "I just wanted to give you my full attention."

What a hypocrite you are, Penny. She speared a tiny piece of pie and hoped her stomach would grow with the task.

The cook smiled coquettishly and ran her hand through her short, tousled hair. "Oh, go ahead and eat! I don't want to be accused of giving you scanty food here at the Grandhotel.

"You really don't have to worry about that," Penny said, "but please continue. Johanna's grandfather, Matthias; a Jewish couple ... what happened next?"

Irmi didn't need to be told twice. "They said they were very rich, this Jewish couple. Jewelers from Vienna or something. They were said to have carried their entire fortune in diamonds."

"And how does your great-aunt know about this old story?"

"She worked here at the hotel back then, as a maid. She's over ninety, you must know." Irmi screwed up her face. "A vicious old hag. And already pretty confused in the head. She claims people disappeared in a cloak-and-dagger operation."

"Who, the Jewish couple?"

"Exactly. Old Matthias is supposed to have betrayed them to the Nazis. Utter nonsense, I tell you. But Leonora claims he went on a search afterwards. For the diamonds the two of them supposedly hid in the hotel. And that he never found the stones."

"So, you think these diamonds might still be here in the house today? "

"I don't. But Great Auntie does. And she's been spreading the story around the village for a few years. Since she became senile. The story gets crazier and crazier, each time she embellishes it even more. Recently, old Matthias is even said to have been her secret lover. Which is complete bullshit. Leonora is a brittle old spinster!"

"But Armin seems to believe her story?"

"Oh yeah. The guy's got a screw loose himself, if you ask me. Sees adventure and mystery everywhere. I'm telling you, he's after the diamonds, even if they don't exist!"

"What did Mrs. Lempra have to say about this story about her grandfather? Did you ever ask her about it?"

"Of course I did. Right after Leonora started spouting that nonsense about Matthias."

"And what did she say?"

"She claimed the Jewish couple was able to flee to the United States. And Matthias is said to have helped them escape the Nazis."

"That means at least this part of the story is true? Mrs. Lempra's grandfather actually hid this couple?"

The cook shrugged. "Why not? I believe the version Johanna told me. She would never have lied to me."

"Maybe she was sugarcoating things a bit? Maybe she was worried about the reputation of the family, or the hotel? A Nazi past doesn't look good at all these days."

"Are you trying to slander her?" the cook demanded.

Penny flashed her a conciliatorily smile. "Not at all. I'm just looking for a motive as to why she was murdered. That's all. We want to catch the killer, don't we?"

Irmi rose from her armchair and came over to Penny. "You make a smart impression, missy. I can see something like that in a minute. Maybe you're a pretty good detective, too. But I'll tell you something: I don't think your services are needed here at the hotel. Johanna will solve this crime herself!"

She fell silent, letting her words sink in, and gave Penny a triumphant look.

"I'm afraid I don't follow," Penny said.

"Johanna was seen in the house, haven't you heard?"

Not that ghost story again. Penny groaned inwardly. "Jakub mentioned it," she said with little enthusiasm. "And Miriam, but she probably had a nightmare."

"What if she didn't? "

"You don't seriously think Mrs. Lempra is haunting the place?" Penny would actually have judged the cook to be a perfectly reasonable woman. One who had both feet firmly on the ground. Should she have been mistaken?

Irmi shook her head briskly. "Don't, Miss, don't be silly. You read too many ghost stories!"

"Then what?" Penny didn't understand anything anymore.

The cook put on her triumphant smile again. She extended her index finger and wagged it in Penny's face. "I'm telling you, she's *alive*!"

"Please what?"

"You want to be a detective? Think Sherlock Holmes! The *Reichenbach Fall*, does that ring any bells?" More triumphant grinning, coupled with the condescending look of a head teacher struggling with a particularly obtuse student.

Of course, Penny knew the Sherlock Holmes story, in which the master detective apparently died—only to reappear years later, very much alive and kicking. But Irmi couldn't seriously be suggesting that Johanna Lempra had performed a similar stunt? Sherlock Holmes was a book character!

Penny shook her head unwillingly. "You think Johanna *faked* her death?"

Irmi nodded. "She's doing the same as Sherlock Holmes. She makes the murderer think she's dead and haunts the hotel to draw him out. To make him slip up and give himself away. Maybe she even wants to get him to try to kill her again. So she can catch him red-handed. Isn't that what you call it? Johanna is very brave, you know. Always has been. You can't falter if you want to stop evil!"

"And you think Johanna wouldn't know who tried to kill her if she was actually still alive?", Penny asked. "That she'd have to find out by playing games with her killer?"

She couldn't believe she was seriously having this discussion. Often, she was accused of having too vivid an imagination—but this cook easily outshone her.

"Why don't you use your head, Miss," Irmi reprimanded her. "Johanna was pushed down the stairs.

Pushed from behind. All right? She couldn't recognize her killer then. Even if she didn't die, she certainly lost consciousness. The fall down the stairs must have been terribly painful for her."

"What about the death certificate?" Penny pointed out. "Do you think the doctor who issued it wouldn't have noticed if Johanna had still been alive? Or the mortician who buried her?"

"Ha!" it came promptly from Irmi. "They're good friends of Johanna's, the two of them! Both Dr. Schopp and old man Gergow. They're in cahoots with her, of course! Besides, Johanna was cremated. So there was no problem about a missing body in the grave. To get a heap of ashes, you can burn all sorts of things, can't you?"

She looked at Penny in silence for a moment—presumably savoring her triumph. Then she narrowed her eyes conspiratorially. "I'm telling you, the murderer had better watch out! Johanna will hunt him down, you'll see."

12

Armin and Wilhelm were already sitting in the hotel's breakfast room when Penny showed up there shortly after eight in the morning.

Each of the men had settled at his own table. Penny headed for a third, directly in front of one of the panorama windows with a view of the valley. Wilhelm gave her a friendly nod of greeting, while Armin's attention was entirely devoted to Miriam.

Apparently, breakfast service was also one of Miriam's duties at the hotel. She was wearing a lace apron and was pouring Armin steaming hot coffee. And making eyes at him in the process.

"Would you like to come along today?" he asked her after she had added fresh rolls to his bread basket. "I want to go to the old elementary school this afternoon, take some pictures. You've got to see it. The light, the atmosphere ... it's like a place from another world."

Miriam squinted over at Penny. "Are you going to need me all day? Or could I—"

"Go ahead," Penny said quickly. "There are a few points I'd like to clear up with you, but after that I'll manage on my own."

Armin leaned over and grinned patronizingly at Penny. "How's our detective doing this morning?" he asked in a joking tone. "Catch the killer yet? No? Well, no wonder, because let me tell you something: there is no killer "

Miriam looked at him in irritation. "And the break-in?" she asked. "How do you explain it if Grandma really just had an accident?"

Armin pulled his shoulders up. "Admittedly, a strange coincidence that this happened now of all times. The crime rate here in your delightful end of the world is certainly not high."

He grinned at Miriam. "But maybe that's why a burglar tried his luck for once? The guy must have been an amateur anyway. I mean, who would think of targeting such a run-down shack, of all things?"

When he saw Miriam frowning, he quickly added, "I just want don't want you to be frightened anymore! That you stop this ridiculous murder hunt and turn back to the living. To me, for example." His grin grew even wider.

After breakfast, Penny followed the young hotel manager into the small office behind the reception desk. Once there, Miriam booted up the computer on which the Grandhotel's guest data was stored.

The computer looked as if it was from the last millennium. It rattled, groaned, and beeped, and it took ten minutes before the startup screen was visible.

"What do you know about Christiane Wittmann?" Penny repeated the question that had led them both here.

Miriam scanned through the guest file on the screen.

"The address she gave is in Linz. She's 53 years old, widowed ... but we already knew that. Do you think she really poisoned her husband?"

"And her son-in-law, too, if your grandma was right," Penny said.

Miriam screwed up her face and continued clicking through the info on the screen. "That's odd," she said a moment later. "I can't find a room bill for Mrs. Wittmann anywhere here."

"Could your grandmother have forgotten to save the bill?"

"I'm sure she didn't. I already told you how meticulous she was. She checked every receipt three times. If there's no invoice on file here, then she didn't issue one."

"Then I guess we have to assume that Mrs. Wittmann left without paying."

Miriam nodded hesitantly. "Oh God, Penny, surely she murdered Grandma! Otherwise, she would have checked out properly, right?"

"And after that she returned to break into your grandmother's archive—she didn't even know existed? And she tore up the diaries, only to leave the pages in place where Johanna accuses her of murder?"

Miriam looked at her with wide eyes. "That doesn't make any sense," she whispered.

"Not really," Penny said. Or had they missed something? She skimmed the data again that Miriam had brought up on the screen. "The name listed there under *miscellaneous*, Jacqueline Wittmann, who is that? The daughter?"

Miriam frowned. "I think ... oh yeah, wait, she was here once. At the very beginning, a week or so after Christiane checked in with us. I've forgotten all about that. We talked briefly. She was worried about her mother who isolated herself here after Mr. Wittmann died. She left her phone number and asked me to keep an eye on Christiane. I should call her right away if her mother became depressed or something. She gave me a very generous tip."

"But you never called her?"

"There was no reason for it. Christiane liked to keep to herself, but she didn't seem unhappy or even depressed. She acted perfectly normal, for someone who has lost a loved one—" She interrupted herself. "Gosh, Penny, she didn't love him at all. She killed him in cold blood!"

"If your grandmother was right—"

"Oh, she certainly was. She was almost never wrong. And Christiane just disappeared without paying! The day Grandma died! How much more proof do you need!"

"I think I should give this Jacqueline Wittmann a call," Penny said. "Would you mind if I pretended to be an employee of the hotel?"

"What, no, of course not. But what are you going to do?"

Half an hour later, Penny sat on the bed in her room and switched off her cell phone. She had just finished the phone call with Christiane Wittmann's daughter.

Jacqueline knew nothing about the fact that her mother had disappeared from Mönchswald. At least that's what she had claimed, and she had seemed so alarmed that Penny was inclined to believe her.

"Left two weeks ago?" she had repeated several times, sounding more hysterical each time. "And you don't know where she went?"

"I was hoping you could tell us, Jacqueline."

"Me? No! Oh God, something must have happened to her! Mama didn't like to travel, you know. She hardly ever left Linz when Papa was alive. She was very attached to him, and his loss must have hit her terribly. So I let her have her way when she insisted on moving to Mönchswald for a while. She was very happy there in her youth, although I don't know the details. They say you have to give people time to grieve, don't they? And that everyone must handle the big losses in life in their own way. I would have liked to have Mom around, but she wanted to be alone. I accepted that. But now ... oh God, I have to report her missing right away!"

"Um, could you keep us updated at the Hotel Mönchswald, please? If your mother shows up again? She wasn't just a guest for us, you know. She was a friend of my employer—who recently passed away herself."

Sometimes you had to creatively extend the truth. "We'd like to know if your mother is all right. Hopefully she'll turn up soon."

"Yes, yes of course," Jacqueline stammered. "And my condolences, about your employer!"

Penny leaned against the head of the bed and closed her eyes. She didn't like this Christiane Wittmann affair at all. But was it really as simple as Miriam assumed?

Was this woman Johanna's murderer?

Penny wasn't so sure about that, but the missing person's report that Jacqueline Wittmann wanted to file was helpful in any case. The police would be looking for Christiane now. That was a start.

In the meantime, there were other leads to follow. So many at once that Penny didn't know where to start. Of the clues she had uncovered so far, one sounded crazier than the next. A murdered Jewish couple from the Nazi-era. Diamonds that were supposed to be hidden somewhere within the old walls of the Grandhotel. Johanna Lempra, who was supposedly haunting the house, either as a ghost or even in the flesh, having faked her own death.

Penny decided to start with Armin Keyser. It couldn't hurt to take a closer look at this lost places researcher. At least you didn't need an exorcist to do that.

She jumped off the bed, picked up her laptop, which she had stored in the clothes chest, and settled down at the desk. When she typed *Armin Keyser, lost places,* into the search engine, it spit out Armin's website in third place.

Penny clicked on the link.

Armin's web presence was professionally designed. The images and layout exuded an aura of mystery, stirring a longing for adventure in the viewer. Mr. Keyser staged himself as a kind of modern Indiana Jones. *The world is full of wonders,* was a quote from him, prominently displayed on the landing page.

Further down was the motto to which he was committed in his exploration of lost places. His code of honor, as he called it wholeheartedly: *Take nothing but photos, leave nothing but footprints!*

That didn't sound much like someone who murdered an old woman because there might have been a Nazi-era treasure hidden in her hotel. In the form of diamonds …

Penny clicked on the tab labeled *Publications* and scrolled through the books that had been penned by Armin.

Underground Vienna.

Mysterious Waldviertel.

99 Scary Places in Tyrol.

99 Forgotten Places in Styria.

And now he had set his sights on Lower Austria. Nothing unusual about it. Perhaps he really had extended his stay at the Grandhotel Mönchswald for a completely harmless reason. Because he liked the atmosphere? Well, and Miriam. But there was nothing criminal about that.

On the other hand, Armin was obviously snooping around the house. Even at night; at least that's what the janitor had claimed, who for his part liked to stick his nose into other people's business. Besides, Penny herself had discovered dirt on Armin's clothes on the evening of her arrival. And dust on his shoes.

He had been hanging around in places where no one had cleaned for a long time. In forgotten, abandoned places. And perhaps not just to snap a few photos. Maybe he had even dug somewhere and got the dirt marks under his otherwise so well-kept fingernails.

Penny had to think of the strange story Irmi had told her. About the two Jewish refugees who carried their fortune in diamonds and had found a hiding place here in the hotel during the war years. Only to be betrayed by Johanna's grandfather to the Nazis shortly afterward? For the sake of their treasure?

And then there was the cryptic entry in Johanna's diary. *Armin can't fool me; he's not really interested in Miriam. I have to protect her from him.*

What exactly had she wanted to protect her granddaughter from? From a broken heart? Or from something much worse?

13

In the afternoon, Penny took another look at Johanna Lempra's archive. Miriam had gone to Aspern to buy supplies for the weekend, and had an appointment with Armin afterwards. But that was just fine with Penny, so she could delve into the old master detective's diaries undisturbed and at her leisure.

If she managed to better understand how Johanna Lempra had worked, if she could learn more about her investigative methods, follow her trains of thought, then maybe she had a chance to track down the old lady's killer.

This time Penny focused on the older diaries, the ones that didn't have any pages missing.

Here, too, Johanna had kept careful records of her thoughts, her cases, and made the occasional note about her family life. Mostly, she had written down something about Miriam; worries or even joyful events, things that filled her with pride.

Nowhere, however, did Penny find any reference to the strange letter Johanna had left for her granddaughter. Not a word about when the master sleuth had written those lines. Or even what had motivated her to do so.

Learn from the past, my beloved Miriam, and you will never be a beggar again.

What had the old woman wanted to tell her granddaughter and heiress with these strange words? What was Miriam supposed to learn from the past? Something that was found here in the archive?

The fact that Johanna had left the letter in her desk didn't have to mean anything. It might merely have been placed with other important documents.

Penny must have run the words through her head half a dozen times before finally giving up on them. This particular mystery would have to wait, if it was one at all.

She turned back to the diaries. Almost as numerous as the passages about Miriam were entries concerning Wilhelm Lindner. Penny got the impression that he must have been more than just a friend to the old lady. Johanna had often thought of him, taken a lively interest in his life and dedicated many pages of her diaries to him.

In addition, these older notebooks were also full of pasted photographs and newspaper clippings. They contained transcripts of conversations Johanna had had with the witnesses and suspects in her murder cases, as well as solutions to detective stories the old lady had read or watched on TV.

It would be fascinating to publish these diaries, Penny thought. There had been a number of famous diarists in literary history: Anne Frank on the Holocaust, Anaïs Nin on her love life. Goethe's sister, Marilyn Monroe ...

The diaries of Johanna Lempra were just as unique in their own way—surely crime fiction lovers around the world would be only too eager to devour these texts.

Penny became engrossed in the criminal cases Johanna

had solved. Miriam's grandmother had traveled all over Europe, and it seemed that crime had followed her everywhere. Or rather, no matter where she was, the old lady had always picked up the trail of murderers—even if she had merely had a harmless week's vacation on the Mediterranean in mind.

Her methods had not been those described in modern textbooks of criminology. Johanna had solved her crimes with a mixture of shrewdness, common sense and female intuition. She had relied on close observation, patience, curiosity, seemingly innocuous conversations in the neighborhood, and an excellent gossip network that seemed to reach beyond the country's borders.

After the respective crime was solved, however, words of disillusionment often followed, sometimes even of bitterness. Johanna had only rarely succeeded in handing over the culprit or culprits to the police and actually getting them convicted. The vast majority of cases came to nothing—if one looked at them soberly.

Sometimes Johanna's account simply ended with the murderer having moved away and she had lost sight of him. Sometimes a higher justice seemed to be at work, and Johanna noted in her diary that a poisoner had had an accident herself, or a patricide had succumbed to a fatal illness. In each of these cases, the old lady had pasted a devotional picture into her diary. Portraits of saints, of the Mother of God, of Jesus ...

The Lord is our judge, could often be found in Johanna's pin-sharp writing at the end of a criminal case. Apparently, the master detective had been a devout Christian who trusted that in the end everyone would receive their just reward. The good as well as the evil ones.

The more notebooks Penny looked through, the more often she noticed the images of saints. Apparently, quite a few of Johanna's murderers had not gotten away with their crimes after all, even if they had managed to evade the secular authorities. The God Miriam's grandmother had worshipped was obviously a merciless judge.

When Penny made her way back to her room, it was already pitch dark outside. She ran down the stairs, rummaged the brass key with the old-fashioned tassel out of her handbag—and stopped abruptly. A glimmer of light could be seen in the narrow gap under her bedroom door.

Strange. She hadn't turned on any lights when she had been here briefly at noon. Or had she?

She tiptoed up to the door, got down on her knees—and peered through the keyhole.

Jakub? From the looks of it, the janitor was busy rummaging through her dresser. Which was definitely not a maid's job.

Resolutely, she pushed down the door handle and thrust the door open. Jakub cringed with a hushed scream.

The next moment, however, he had already regained his composure. Calmly, he slid shut the drawer he had just disappeared into up to his elbows and gave Penny a wry smile. "No offense," he said, "I just wanted to make sure."

"That I keep my dresser in good order, or what?" Penny retorted. The curiosity of this man was really pathological.

He straightened up to his full height—which did not make a very imposing impression.

"Mrs. Lempra had many enemies," he announced. "In Vienna, even—and much further afield. And they may now be after Miss Miriam, too. I'm the only one in the house who can protect her! I'm just doing my duty!"

"Protect Miriam? From me?" asked Penny in disbelief.

Jakub narrowed his eyes. "Who's going to tell us that you're really a detective? That you didn't deliberately approach Miss Miriam to—" He faltered.

"To what?" asked Penny sharply. "To rob her? Murder her?"

The janitor stiffened. "You can never be too careful!" he proclaimed, already sounding far less confident in the hero's role he had ascribed to himself.

Penny pointed to her dresser. "And did you find any pertinent evidence in my underwear? That I'm a spy or even a murderer?"

He twisted the corners of his mouth, rubbing his pointed nose in embarrassment.

"I'll stay alert," he announced in lieu of an answer. And then he made off as fast as his short legs would carry him.

14

The next morning, right after breakfast, Penny slipped into her winter boots and the warm jacket she had brought with her to Mönchswald. Then she set off on her way. She walked the short distance up the mountain that Irmi, the cook, had described to her.

Irmi's great-aunt Leonora lived in a small cottage right next to the cemetery. And that, in turn, was located next to the town's tiny church, which you couldn't miss—according to Irmi.

An icy wind whistled around Penny's ears, and dark clouds gathered in the sky, heralding snow. In this weather, Mönchswald seemed more deserted than ever.

On her way she did not meet a single person. But at least, thanks to Irmi's description, she found the great-aunt's house without any problems. She wanted to get an impression of the old woman who had told Armin Keyser the story about the missing diamonds.

Leonora didn't have a telephone, but the cook had assured Penny that she would have no trouble getting in if she went to see the old witch in person. That was Irmi's affectionate term for her great-aunt.

"Leonora is delighted to welcome anyone who comes to see her, and whose ears she can talk off. If you like, feel free to say that I sent you."

Armed with this recommendation, Penny pressed the bell button next to the front door. The door of the small cottage was opened not three seconds later—and out peeked an old woman.

Penny hesitated. The term *old woman* was certainly appropriate, but the lady who had opened the door to her was definitely not ninety years old. More like seventy. "Can I help you?" the woman asked, not unkindly.

Penny gave her name, referred to the Grandhotel cook, and then asked if Irmi's great-aunt Leonora was available.

As it turned out, the woman at the door was named Erika and was the old lady's daughter-in-law.

"Leonora has fallen ill," she announced, "that's why I'm here. I'm taking care of her. She must have upset her stomach last night, pretty bad. Well, I'd rather spare you the details, but I'm afraid you'll have to come back some other time."

A sudden illness? Penny's suspicions were immediately aroused. Leonora might have been nothing more than the old gossip her great-niece had described her as—but she might also have been an important witness in a murder case. And thus in danger herself, because she knew too much?

But the daughter-in-law didn't seem particularly concerned about the old lady.

"She'll be fine," she said, "she's tough as hell."

She eyed Penny silently for a moment, then asked, "What is this all about? Why do you want to speak to

Leonora?"

Penny hesitated for a moment, but then concluded that Erika was probably her best chance for more information at the moment.

"It's about Armin Keyser; he's also a hotel guest. He recently spoke to your mother-in-law about ... well, the past."

Erika looked almost disappointed. "Oh yes, he was here because of that old matter from the war that Leonora has been so eager to gossip about lately. She loves to play herself up as a contemporary witness, you know. Especially since her memory is going downhill. She's spent her whole life here in this backwater, can you imagine? She must be dying of boredom, that's why she's telling these stories—that's what I always say to my Hans. But Leonora is his mother, he loves her ... and he doesn't have to listen to her tales. He is at work most of the time, my Hans, while I take care of the household. Well, and his Mama. So, if you want to hear my opinion: don't give a damn about Leonora's stories."

"But Mr. Keyser was interested in what your mother-in-law had to say, I suppose?" asked Penny. She stepped from one foot to the other. Slowly it was getting quite cold out here, despite the thick jacket.

Erika reacted promptly. "Well, where are my manners? Letting you freeze to death here! Why don't you come in and warm up a bit?"

Penny didn't need to be told twice. She was led into a spacious room that seemed to be both kitchen and living area. The ceiling hung low, and the sofa where Erika let her take a seat was scuffed and a little stained.

But then, out of nowhere, Leonora's daughter-in-law conjured up a delicious cup of hot chocolate, which she also enhanced with fresh whipped cream. Just the thing on a frosty winter's day.

"Yes, well, as far as Mr. Keyser is concerned," Erika resumed the conversation after settling down across from Penny. "He did indeed seem very interested. Amazing, isn't it? He acted like he gave a damn about Leonora's diatribes. Listened to her for hours; no idea where he got the patience. And he's such a good-looking man, don't you think?"

"Yeah, huh," Penny said. "How did the two of them meet? Armin and your mother-in-law?"

"I have no idea, he just showed up here. I happened to be here that afternoon, too. I'm doing the shopping for Leonora, you know. And cleaning up a little bit around here. She just can't manage it anymore."

Penny looked at her expectantly, so she continued speaking. "Mr. Keyser said he had been researching the town archive. For his new book. He's a famous author, isn't he? And he seemed to be well informed, about the history of Mönchswald. I don't know who would want to read about a backwater like ours. Well, anyway, apparently someone recommended Leonora to him as a possible source. I think that's how he put it. He asked her lots of questions, for hours. And she liked that, I tell you. She talked and talked and talked."

"And what specifically did they talk about?" asked Penny.

Erika tilted her head and scrutinized her. "Are you a writer, too?" she asked, suddenly suspicious.

"No," Penny said quickly. "Just a friend of Miriam's. But I'm, uh, interested in history, too, you know. And Irmi already told me the story about the Jewish couple, if that's what it was about ..."

"Oh, I see. Right. Well, it's no secret, I guess. Leonora tells everyone who wants to know anyway. And everybody else too. But she embellishes the story a bit more each time, it seems to me. She told Mr. Keyser a real spine-chiller. She claimed that old Matthias didn't betray this Jewish couple to the Nazis during the Second World War. But that he killed them himself, both of them, in order to get hold of their diamonds. He is said to have murdered them at night and then buried them in the forest. Leonora claims to have found poorly cleaned traces of blood the next morning while tidying up, and of course she approached him about it. Supposedly she was even his mistress at the time—and that's why he confessed everything to her. Which is complete humbug, if you ask me."

"Did your mother-in-law ever get to see these diamonds for herself?" asked Penny.

"No way."

"And she only started spreading this story in the recent past? Did I understand that correctly?"

Erika nodded. "I once asked her why she's coming out with it now of all times, half a century later. I'll tell you it's because she's going senile and wants to give herself airs. But she emphasized she didn't want to hurt Johanna. Nor the reputation of the hotel. She told Mr. Keyser however, that in the 21st century one should finally be able to speak openly about the past. The way she put it, not everything was bad back then with the Nazis. Can you imagine that? I wanted to die of shame!"

After Penny had thanked Erika and left the little cottage behind, she headed home.

The sky looked a bit friendlier, the clouds had dispersed, and the wind didn't feel quite so icy anymore either.

Penny's head was full of questions. She couldn't even tell if she had learned anything important in the conversation with Erika. Something that would let her make progress in the Johanna Lempra murder case.

As she passed the old cemetery wall, crumbling in many places and overgrown with ivy, she spotted a familiar figure on the opposite side of the street. Wilhelm Lindner was just climbing out of his car—with a huge bouquet of dark red roses in his arms.

He didn't seem to notice Penny, but headed straight for the cemetery. He passed through the wrought-iron gate, which was still in remarkably good shape, at least compared to the enclosure or even the graves, most of which were overgrown.

Penny had wanted to return to the hotel directly, but now her curiosity was aroused. Whose grave was Wilhelm Lindner visiting here at the cemetery? With a bouquet of flowers that would be appropriate for a golden wedding anniversary?

She took cover at a half-ruined house just to the right of the cemetery's main entrance. An old rectory? Or once the residence of the cemetery keeper?

It would certainly have made a fantastic photo subject for Armin. It looked as if it had sprung from Grimm's fairy tales. A real-life enchanted cottage at the edge of the forest, lonely and left to decay. And right next to it the graves, which seemed just as abandoned and forgotten.

The door of the old building hung on its hinges as if it could fall out at any moment. The lower windows were nailed shut with wooden boards; those on the upper floor were missing the panes. This house had to be a popular meeting place at night for the young people of the area. If there were any youngsters left in Mönchswald at all.

Penny suddenly had to think back to her own school days. Not far from the elite boarding school where her mother had sent her for a few years, there had been an old, long-abandoned cemetery. How many nights had she stolen out of her room to sneak smokes with boys of higher grades ... or later to make out with them.

The dark and mysterious had always magically attracted her. And the forbidden even more so. She had not chosen it; she was born that way.

"Why can't I have a normal girl for a daughter?" her mother had lamented all too often.

And now here she was, finally disowned and disinherited by Frederike Küfer, working her second murder case—still during her training period at the detective academy.

I love my life, she thought—then she hurried to follow Wilhelm unobtrusively.

He headed straight for a grave with a marble angel hovering over it, knelt there and placed the lush bouquet of roses at the statue's feet. Then he kissed his own fingertips and pressed them tenderly on the stone tomb slab.

He remained for a long time, motionless, his head lowered on his chest, and seemed to hold intimate communion with the deceased.

When he finally rose, Penny ducked behind the nearest tombstone. He left without turning around again. In his hand, he carried a bouquet of roses as large as the one he had brought with him. Only this one had wilted, and Wilhelm disposed of it in the trash can near the exit. Apparently, it had not been his first visit to this grave.

When he was long gone, Penny left her hiding place and ran over to the angel at whose feet he had knelt.

Several names were engraved on the tombstone under the heavenly creature. The last one, at the very bottom, set in fresh gold letters, read: *Johanna Lempra*.

15

After Penny returned to the hotel, she decided to extend her stay in Mönchswald. Although tomorrow was Monday, and she would have to skip classes at Argus Academy.

She hadn't missed a day since the beginning of her training, so she could allow herself to take a few days off sick. Here, in this so-called lost place, something strange was going on. She sensed danger, even if she couldn't say for whom and for what reason.

But hadn't even a detective as experienced as Johanna Lempra often relied on her intuition? Vague as it might be? And there was nothing but boring stuff on the agenda for next week's course anyway. The third part of legal studies, and already modules one and two had almost put her into a coma. As it turned out, absolutely everything that was fun was forbidden to an Austrian professional detective.

After a quick dinner at the hotel restaurant, Penny buried herself in Johanna Lempra's archive again.

As she made herself comfortable on the flower-patterned velvet sofa and began to browse several more of the old lady's diaries, she was overcome by a guilty conscience. What was she actually doing here? Was this really serving the case? Was it helping her in her murder investigation? Or was studying these books nothing more than indulging in extremely fascinating reading?

A mystery treat at the Grandhotel.

Penny pushed the thought aside. You're just being thorough, she told herself. Maybe she would find the crucial clue in those books after all. Very soon. You never knew.

She had always been a true master in the art of justifying certain actions to herself. Things she wanted to do, no matter how unnecessary or even reprehensible they might be.

At first, she found nothing in the old diaries that would have justified her spending hours in the archives. Only page after page in Johanna Lempra's immaculate handwriting. Poison murders, murders disguised as accidents or as strange illnesses, revenge murders, murders out of jealousy and greed for money ... and a great many devotional pictures that Johanna had pasted between the pages whenever a murderer himself had come to his death. Be it through an accident, an illness ... or through circumstances that remained unclear.

Really a lot of devotional pictures, it went through Penny's mind at some point. And of the remaining murderers, those who did not die, a striking number had moved away—or simply disappeared.

Was she already getting paranoid, or were there actually more deaths among these criminals than could be explained statistically? And also far too many relocations, moves or the like? Then again, the latter could be explained somehow, if these people were really murderers. That one or the other of them no longer wanted to live in the place where he had committed his crime was all too understandable.

Johanna herself had apparently not found this strange. Nowhere had Miriam's grandmother said a word about the fact that the death rate among her murderers seemed unusually high to her. At least Penny couldn't find any such remark. This might have been because there were always enough new cases to occupy the attention of the passionate amateur detective.

Had Johanna, whose whole interest was in violent deaths, simply no longer had a feeling for how high the natural mortality rate was in a country like Austria? Or was there another explanation ... a far less innocuous one?

While studying the diaries, Penny discovered a second thing that struck her as odd. Next to some passages about Miriam, Johanna had drawn a tiny symbol with a fountain pen.

It consisted of three strokes, a thicker and larger one on the far left and two smaller ones to the right. It was reminiscent of a flame. Penny turned on her cell phone and snapped a photo.

What did this symbol stand for? Was it just a whim of the old lady? A decoration, perhaps?

Unlikely, because otherwise there were no scribbles, no hand-painted sketches or similar in Johanna's diaries. Moreover, the flame symbol only appeared when the corresponding page was about Miriam. And the content of the passages had nothing to do with fire or flames.

Very strange.

The oldest symbol Penny discovered was in a book that dated back just under eight years. Before that, there were no flames, no matter how many books she searched. In the diaries of the last few years, Penny found a total of twelve of the small symbols. What was it all about?

A bloodcurdling scream jolted Penny from her sleep.

She started up, not knowing where she was at first—but then she saw the diary that had just slipped off her lap. She looked around, rubbed her eyes: Johanna Lempra's archive. She had dozed off on the comfortable velvet sofa.

But the scream? Surely, she hadn't dreamed it? It had come from outside, at least that's what Penny thought. Johanna's archive had no balconies, only ordinary windows—but they were old, warped, and leaky. So it was quite possible that she had heard something from outside. The wail of an injured animal? Or whatever else you might hear on a winter night in the foothills of the Alps.

Sleepily, she trotted over to the window, opened it, and looked out. Below her was the parking lot of the Grandhotel, covered by a thin layer of snow. Only a few vehicles were parked there, including her own black kitten.

The ice-cold air that hit her made her eyes water.

Be quick, close the window again!

It was completely quiet out there. Surely, she had only

dreamed the scream.

At that moment she saw it—and was suddenly wide awake. Under one of the balconies of the left side wing something lay in the snow. A metal tube a good ten meters long, it looked like, and half buried under it something Penny could make out much more clearly. A human figure. Motionless, as if taking a nap on the frozen ground.

Penny quickly closed the window, ran to the door, and stormed down the stairs. Once in the foyer, she turned into the hallway that led to the back entrance. To the parking lot. Then she was outside in the open—panting in the freezing cold.

But there was no time for comforts like a warm jacket now. Not twenty meters in front of her lay the human figure, on its stomach, still immobile.

Penny knew this person was dead, lying there all twisted in the snow. It was a woman, for she had long white hair spread out like a fan all around her head, barely standing out against the snow. The metal tube under which she lay buried was a rain gutter, anchored only at its lowest end to the hotel facade. Penny realized that now, too.

She knelt down next to the woman. Who was she? Long white hair? Hadn't Miriam mentioned that her grandmother –

But no, that couldn't be. Johanna Lempra was dead, and had been for two weeks.

Gently, she touched the woman on the shoulder, felt her way up to the neck, looking for a pulse.

Nothing. As she had feared.

With her other hand, she brushed aside a few strands of hair, just enough to make out the face that was half buried in the snow.

The woman's skin looked wrinkled, like that of a very old person—but only at first glance. At second glance, something was wrong. When Penny discovered the brown-pink color on her own fingertips, with which she had just felt the dead woman's neck, she realized what it was: makeup. The wrinkles were merely makeup. An illusion. *What the hell*?

Under the woman's cheek lay a pair of gold-rimmed glasses, completely dented and shattered. Penny bent lower over the dead woman, studied her face—and all at once she recognized who she had before her.

Irmi, the cook. Who was neither a spectacle wearer, nor did she have long white hair. And certainly no wrinkled skin. But obviously she had not only been skillful with the cooking spoon, but also with the makeup brush.

Cautiously, Penny pulled on a strand of hair—and suddenly the whole head seemed to start moving. But that, too, was a deception. Another little tug, and she had the entire head of hair in her hand. Or rather: the wig that Irmi had worn.

Artificial white hair that must have fallen to her hips, plus gold-rimmed glasses. And made-up wrinkles.

In one fell swoop, Penny realized two things:

One, Irmi had dressed up as Johanna Lempra.

And two, she had come to death in that role.

She must have fallen from the balcony above them. From the looks of it, she had tried to climb down the gutter—which had not been up to this load.

The cone of a flashlight suddenly flitted across the ground. Footsteps crunched on the snow. Someone was approaching rapidly.

Then a man's voice called out, "Who's there?"

Penny didn't have to turn around to know who was running toward her. The buzzing voice belonged to Jakub, the janitor.

"It's just me," she said, standing up, with wig still in her hands. "We have to call the police."

16

It was well past midnight when Penny found herself sitting across from a certain Inspector Fleischer of the Aspern Police Department, on the verge of losing her temper.

The conversation took place in the hotel's restaurant, which had long since closed at that time. Nevertheless, all the residents of the hotel had gathered here.

Behind the bar, Miriam was running the coffee maker, while Wilhelm, Jakub and Armin sat around paralyzed, warming their hands and souls on steaming mugs. The shock of Irmi's untimely death was in everyone's bones, and the sight of the corpse was probably still haunting them—even though it had long since been removed by the police.

Inspector Fleischer, on the other hand, looked as if he could hardly wait to return to his warm bed. For him the case was clear, no matter what arguments Penny gave him. In his opinion, Irmi had suffered a tragic accident. There was no evidence of foul play. Therefore, no case for Major Crimes. End of the investigation.

"Dilapidated old shack, this hotel," he grumbled. "You'd have to be crazy to climb down a rain gutter."

"She didn't climb down willingly," Penny said, surely

for the fourth time. "She was on the run! From Johanna Lempra's murderer! You should at least consider the possibility. Investigate this death properly, get your colleagues from Major Crimes involved!"

She had the urgent need to bang her fist on the tabletop to shake up this sleepyhead of a police officer.

But she restrained herself. *Remain professional. Keep your cool.*

Act like a lady, her mother would have added. Damn it, that was easier said than done with this inspector.

Without her being able to stop it, her thoughts wandered back to Jürgen Moser—the police officer she had worked with in her first murder case. Jürgen wasn't only a pretty cute guy in appearance, he also possessed imagination and ambition and wasn't slavishly following the letter of the law. He had at least listened to Penny, as crazy as her theories might have sounded to him.

Inspector Fleischer, on the other hand, had neither charm nor imagination and was about as sweet as a shriveled lemon. An uncreative bore who did his job by the book—and was looking at Penny as if she were an alien.

He had had a few brief conversations with the residents of the house only to come to the following conclusion: Irmi had been unable to cope with the tragic death of her employer and longtime friend, and therefore deluded herself into thinking that she had been murdered. Like Johanna Lempra before her, she began snooping around as an amateur detective in order to hunt down the alleged murderer.

She had even gone so far as to disguise herself as her former boss. She had entered the rooms of the hotel residents on several nights in order to make them believe that the old master sleuth was still alive. In this way, she wanted to lure Johanna's murderer—who, according to Inspector Fleischer, existed only in her imagination—out of hiding.

Sporty as Irmi was, she climbed over balcony gratings and rain gutters on the hotel facade during her nightly appearances. And tonight, one such climbing action had been her undoing. The gutter she was climbing down had ripped from its fixture, and the cook had fallen to her death. Period. The end. Case closed.

"I completely agree with you that Irmi pretended to be Johanna," Penny told the inspector. "She even tried to make me believe that Johanna had only faked her death and was now investigating her own murder. But will you please explain to me why she should be haunting the vacant part of the hotel? There is no inhabited room far and wide where she crashed. She could hardly expect anyone to see her in this side wing."

"She wasn't quite right in the head, haven't you figured that out yet? I have no idea what she was up to." The policeman's patience was clearly nearing its end.

"Surely there are only two reasonable explanations for Irmi's climbing down that gutter," Penny said quickly. "First, she lured Johanna's suspected killer into the abandoned side wing. Maybe she was setting a trap for him. Or second, she was on the run from him. Probably both. In this order. She tried to set a trap for him, but something went wrong, and then she tried to escape via the balcony. And fell off. Or was pushed. The gutter could also have been torn out of its fixture afterwards. To make it look like an accident. That should at least be investigated!"

"You call that a reasonable explanation?", the policeman snorted.

He leaned back and pulled the corners of his mouth into what was probably meant to be a sympathetic smile. "Look, Miss Küfer, I liked Irmi. Honestly. Her schnitzels were to die for. So was her curd strudel. But she wasn't reasonable. She always had all kinds of fluff in her head, almost as bad as Mrs. Lempra when she was alive. And now she dressed up as her dead boss and haunted the place at night! Do you call that sensible, for heaven's sake?"

Penny said nothing in reply.

"And as I have told you repeatedly, no one pushed Irmi", the inspector continued. "On the balcony above, we only found her own footprints in the snow. Don't you understand? No murderer far and wide. She was all alone."

"OK. But she was still on the run. Why else would she have climbed off the balcony in the abandoned side wing? Why not take the stairs? If she had some head start on the killer, maybe he was just reaching the balcony when Irmi fell off. He stopped instead of running after her. Therefore, no trace of him in the snow. Apart from that, these balconies are so narrow that he could have been standing in the doorway and pushed her from

there. No need to step out into the snow at all if he possessed some strength. That would have to be investigated further too!"

"I'm sorry, Miss Küfer. I have to leave now. It's late; we
should all be in bed by now. And if I may give you some
advice: stop suspecting a crime everywhere you go just
because you like to play detective."

Jürgen Moser would never have said something like
that to her.

17

None of the hotel residents wanted to go to sleep, even though it would soon be dawning. After the inspector left the hotel, they gathered in the room on the second floor that had been Johanna Lempra's living room. The small salon had always served as a kind of common room in the hotel.

Wilhelm knelt in front of the open fireplace and stoked the fire. It would have been an exceedingly cozy room if death and fear had not followed them here.

Penny sipped a strong coffee while Miriam stood very close to Armin with a schnaps glass in her hand.

"What do you think?" Penny addressed them. "Was Irmi's death an accident? I'd love to hear your opinions."

She was curious about the reactions. One of these people was responsible for the death of the cook, of that she was sure. They might not have pushed her, but had driven her to her death. Because they had mistaken her for Johanna. Irmi's own cunning had been her undoing.

Jakub was the first to speak. "She was murdered! She found out something, and the murderer silenced her."

Armin groaned. "Guys, please, be reasonable. That inspector was right: you have to stop seeing crime everywhere. Or else it will drive you crazy. Irmi is the best example of that! Dressing up as Johanna and haunting the hotel—how crazy is that? She scared the hell out of

Miriam with her ghost show, didn't she?"

Miriam nodded hesitantly.

"Are you sure it was murder, Miss Küfer?" asked Wilhelm, calmly, measuredly, with a sidelong glance at Miriam.

Penny faltered briefly, then came up with a plan in a flash. It was a completely crazy idea. And dangerous to boot. But as things stood now, it was probably her only chance.

"I'm sure of it," she told Wilhelm. "Irmi was not alone when she died. It may not be murder, legally speaking, if she fell while trying to escape, in that daring climb, but the person who was chasing her is certainly to blame."

But then she turned to Armin. "Irmi wasn't the one haunting the hotel, though. That is, at least not exclusively."

"Excuse me?" asked the lost places researcher. "What's that supposed to mean? Irmi was dressed as Johanna when she died! "

"That's true," Penny replied. "I think she was trying to trap the killer tonight with that costume."

"Oh God," Armin moaned. "I'm tired of listening to this nonsense. You're clearly reading too many crime novels!"

He set his glass down on the mantel and was about to leave the room. But Penny stepped in his way.

"I said *tonight*. Not necessarily on *every* occasion Johanna was seen at the hotel. It wasn't always Irmi. I think she was merely an aide. An ally."

"A what?" Armin and Jakub asked the question almost simultaneously. Even Wilhelm, who had remained inconspicuously in the background until now, raised both eyebrows in surprise.

"I was the first to reach Irmi after she fell from that balcony; you know that," Penny addressed everyone at once. "I found her. And I saw something. Or rather, *someone.*"

She looked at Miriam. "I didn't know your grandmother when she was alive, but there are plenty of photos of her in this house."

"Yes ... and?" asked Miriam, aghast.

"She was there. Alive. At the scene of the crime. She was standing at the edge of the forest, behind the hotel. She looked at me, then disappeared among the trees. I'm sure it was her. Johanna."

The words had not missed their effect. First there were shouts of astonishment and incredulous looks, then Penny was bombarded with questions. But she stuck to her story: Johanna Lempra was alive. A master detective by all accounts, the old lady had concocted a fantastic plot with the parish doctor and the mortician, and had fooled everyone else. Especially the murderer. And Johanna certainly wouldn't rest until she hunted him down. Especially now that he had Irmi's death on his conscience, too.

Penny took advantage of the awkward silence that spread in the room to check the alibis of those present. "Would you please tell me where you each were at the time Irmi died?", she asked the group.

No one answered.

Then Jakub cleared his throat and croaked: "In my room. I was already asleep. But then I heard the scream. That must have been when Irmi –" He hesitated. "When she fell to her death."

That's a lie for sure, Penny told herself. *Asleep, my ass.* The janitor was always snooping around somewhere in the house, and preferably in the middle of the night. She wasn't even sure if this man ever slept at all.

"I was close by, if you must know" said Armin in a condescending tone. "I was capturing the nighttime atmosphere at the old indoor pool. Took a few pictures. Then I also heard the scream, but I didn't know where it came from. That's why I didn't run out to the parking lot right away."

Pictures? So late at night? And shouldn't Armin have already photographed every broom closet after more than a month's stay in the hotel? Did he use the night hours, when supposedly everyone was asleep, to look for the diamonds?

"I've been asleep, too," Miriam said, "and haven't heard a thing."

Penny nodded. "Where is Theo, by the way?" she then asked.

"At his home. He has to get up early again this morning. He only sleeps at my place occasionally, I told you that." She gave Armin a fleeting sideways glance.

"Was he even here yesterday?" Penny asked.

"No," Miriam replied curtly.

Had the two had a fight? Were Theo's days as Miriam's sweetheart numbered, and would Armin soon take his place?

"And you, Mr. Lindner?" Penny turned to the older man. "Where have you been?"

"I'm afraid I've been in bed, too. Alone, of course. No alibi." He smiled meekly.

Shortly thereafter, the group began to disperse. No one seemed to be in the mood for further conversation. Judging by the pinched faces, their heads were full of questions and gloomy thoughts.

But Penny held Miriam back as she tried to leave the room with Armin. "Can I talk to you for a moment, please?" she said.

Miriam nodded hesitantly and said goodbye to Armin. Which seemed to depress her a lot.

Penny waited until the last resident of the house—it was Wilhelm—had finished his drink and said goodbye. Then, without mincing words, she got down to business. "There's something I have to ask you," she began. "You knew your grandmother best of all people, after all."

"I can't believe she's actually still alive," Miriam said promptly. "Why didn't she let me in on it, then? It's cruel, isn't it, to make me think she's dead when in fact she's—"

"I'm sure she only did it to protect you," Penny interrupted her.

Without giving her client time for further interjections, she got down to the topic that was on her mind.

"I noticed something in your grandmother's diaries that I would like to hear your opinion on," she began— to prepare Miriam for the question she was going to ask her next. A question she would definitely not like.

"My opinion?" echoed Miriam, "about what?"

"About the extremely high rate of accidents, early deaths, or just plain disappearances among the killers your grandmother exposed."

Miriam looked at her with wide eyes. "I don't understand. What are you trying to say?"

"Well," Penny began cautiously, "couldn't it be that your grandmother sometimes, shall we say, took justice into her own hands? I imagine it would be very frustrating if she solved a murder case, but then the police didn't believe her, and the perpetrator got away with it."

Such an accusation could hardly be made more gently, but still Miriam did not take it well. Her expression darkened abruptly.

"Are you crazy?" she blurted out. "You think my grandma was a vigilante, or what? She would never have done anything like that! She never put herself above the law, even though she often got angry with the police. She was very religious and trusted that God would judge the murderers. She always emphasized that. And she firmly believed it."

Miriam glowered angrily at Penny. "You're wrong!" she insisted.

"It was just a question, nothing more. I just wanted to get your opinion. And I think you're right."

Penny had to think of the devotional pictures that Johanna had pasted in her journals. An intercession for the most evil people who walked on God's earth, a request for purification of their souls? But also, at the same time, a thanksgiving for the divine justice that had been done to them, when they, for their part, had departed this life?

Be that as it may, there was no getting around the fact: the death rate among these criminals was far too high. This could not be a coincidence—nor a religious phenomenon. But a very earthly one.

"If Johanna didn't judge these murderers, who did?" she turned back to Miriam.

Her client was clearly not interested in continuing this conversation any longer. "I'm going to bed," she announced, already trying to push past Penny.

"Wait, Miriam, that's not how it works. You do realize I had to ask you that question, right? If we're going to understand what's going on here at the hotel. Why your grandmother was murdered."

"She's not dead at all," Miriam returned bitingly. "That's what you said just now! And you're certainly not going to find her killer by insinuating that she executed people herself. Even if they were criminals. You're barking up the wrong tree. I don't want to listen to this. Good night."

"There's something else I wanted to ask you," Penny said softly. She put one hand on Miriam's arm while she dug her cell phone out of her pocket with the other.

She turned on the device and pressed the icon that linked to her photo album. Then she showed Miriam the photograph she had taken earlier in Johanna Lempra's archive. The little flame icon that had appeared repeat-edly in the diaries whenever Johanna had devoted her-self to her granddaughter.

"Does this ring a bell?" she asked Miriam, "Do you know this symbol?"

Miriam glanced at it. "Hm, I don't know. Looks kind of familiar to me. I think I saw it somewhere recently."

"Outside of your grandmother's journals?"

"Yes ... yes. You know I haven't read her journals."

Penny looked at her expectantly, but that was all Mir-iam had to say. She merely shrugged her shoulders, then grumbled a rather unfriendly "Good night," and left the room.

This time, Penny didn't hold her back.

She returned to her own room, made herself comfort-able in the decrepit bed—and lay awake for a long time.

Relentlessly, all kinds of thoughts bombarded her. All the murder cases she had read about in Johanna Lem-pra's diaries haunted her mind. She had to think again of the many dead or missing, among the criminals the old lady had exposed. And of the pious devotional pic-tures, which did not jibe at all with the shrewdness of a master detective.

Then the sight of the dead cook forced itself before her inner eye. Irmi, disguised with wig and glasses, buried under the gutter in the snow.

And that was not all. There was also Christiane Witt-mann, who had left the hotel without paying, on the very day Johanna had died. And Jakub, the janitor, who was snooping around on his own just as Irmi had done.

Wilhelm Lindner, who carried huge bouquets of flowers to Johanna's grave, and Theo, who was a rather unpleasant fellow. Armin, who was hitting on Miriam and yet at the same time had pestered Irmi's great-aunt about diamonds that were perhaps only a legend.

Like a ghostly parade, they all moved through Penny's mind, which simply didn't want to come to rest.

And then there was the lie that she herself had put into the world—or rather taken over from Irmi and spun on: that Johanna Lempra was still alive.

She had followed a spontaneous impulse when she had made this claim in front of the assembled hotel residents. But now, in the strange state between waking and sleeping, an idea began to form in her head how this lie could be used concretely. To get one step closer to Johanna's murderer.

Just make sure you don't get too close to him in the end, a warning inner voice whispered to her. *You know the price Irmi paid for that.*

18

The next morning, there was a depressing silence in the breakfast room. Wilhelm was munching on a buttered bun, Miriam was busily scurrying around, but without her usual smile on her face, and not even Armin made any effort to flirt with her.

But at least Miriam's anger at Penny seemed to have dissipated. On the contrary, as obliging as she was in serving Penny breakfast and pouring coffee, she must have felt guilty.

"I was a little rough on you last night," she finally said when the two men had already left the breakfast room. "Sorry, Penny, you were just doing your job."

"It's OK," Penny said. "Sometimes asking unpleasant questions is just part of the deal."

Miriam's fiancé, however, who unexpectedly knocked on the door of Penny's room shortly after noon, or rather drummed his fists against it, was not in a conciliatory mood.

Penny had barely opened the door to him when he stormed into the room, venting his anger.

"This has got to stop!" he roared. "Now! I'm not going to let you drive Miriam completely insane!"

"May I offer you a drink?" said Penny calmly—even though there was no minibar in the old-fashioned hotel room and her hospitable feelings toward this guy were severely limited. The manners of this troll could only be met with the grace of a true lady.

Theo looked at her in confusion.

"What? no! I don't want a drink; I want you to leave Miriam alone! Did you really talk her into believing that her grandmother is still alive? And that in addition to being such a snoop, the old woman was lynching people?"

"Those were not quite the words I chose, and I merely put the lynching thing out there as a possibility –"

"You're out of your mind," Theo cut her off. "You're a case for the nuthouse!"

"Where were you last night, anyway?" asked Penny without blinking an eye. "Shall we say around midnight? When Irmi died."

"What?!" Theo puffed himself up even more menacingly. Soon he would explode like a firecracker. "None of your business at all, but I was at home, in Neunkirchen! If you think you can pin something on me –"

"Why, no," Penny said. "You're an honorable citizen, that's totally obvious. I can see that kind of thing immediately. You would never commit murder!"

"You're damn right!"

She enjoyed grounding this troll, playing with him, countering him with irony that he didn't even catch— but she mustn't overdo it. This Theo *was* dangerous. A nasty choleric who couldn't control himself one bit.

He was not very intelligent, but he had plenty of muscle power. No denying that. It could end up very painful to mess with such a guy.

She struck a more conciliatory tone. "I'm almost at the end of my investigation," she lied, "so you'll be rid of me soon."

"That's all right, then," grumbled Theo, already turning to leave. Apparently, he had let off enough steam for now.

But Penny held him back. "Wait," she said, "you could help me clear up one important question."

"What kind of question?" He stared at her suspiciously.

"Like I said, you're not a murderer—but I need to be able to cross a certain item off my list, OK? That argument you had with Johanna, the day she died, what was that about? Surely something quite innocuous, right?" She forced herself to smile beguilingly—which bounced off Theo.

His shoulders twitched. As did his massive upper arms. Had she just triggered his next angry outburst?

Surprisingly though, Miriam's fiancé deigned to make a statement. He cleared his throat, then twisted the corners of his mouth and said, "I don't like the fact that certain people are staying in the house. That's what the conversation with Johanna was about."

Penny looked at him askance. "You interfered with the hotel business? "

"Pah! hotel business. I told the old lady to finally get rid of that pseudo Indiana Jones who's stalking Miriam. That's all."

"Hmm, you're talking about Armin? You were going to get Miriam's grandma to kick him out? Seriously? One of the few paying guests of the hotel?"

"You don't believe me? You think I care?"

Penny pondered. She had the impression that Theo was telling the truth. He was certainly not a gifted liar; he clearly lacked the necessary brains.

Besides, trying to get rid of his rival in such a surreptitious way was quite in line with his character. Instead of treating Miriam so lovingly that she would be completely aloof to the charms of other men.

For a moment they stood facing each other in silence. "Would it reassure you," Penny then said, "if I told you that Armin isn't after your fiancée at all?"

"Oh, yeah? What else?"

She shrugged. "Let's just say he's pursuing other interests at the hotel."

Theo wrinkled his nose. "You think you're pretty smart, don't you?"

Compared to you, for sure, Penny thought, but said nothing. What did such a lovely woman like Miriam see in a guy like that?

"I take it Johanna had no intention of making Armin leave the hotel, right?" she asked. "She must have been happy to have any paying guest. No matter why he extended his stay here."

Theo snorted. "She wouldn't hear of it. But believe me, I would have convinced her yet. And now I'm going to get Miriam to make that guy leave. Mark my words, you'll see!"

19

In the middle of the night, there was another knock at Penny's door. She snapped out of her sleep—and realized it wasn't the middle of the night at all. It was still light outside, and she was lying on the bed fully dressed. She must have dozed off shortly after she'd got rid of Theo.

Great, there's a murderer on the loose in the hotel, and Miss Super Detective is taking a nice little siesta.

She rubbed the sleep from her eyes, then hurried to the door and yanked it open.

Outside stood Miriam, who literally jumped into the room as soon as Penny opened. She seemed to have something on her mind that couldn't wait. Something positive for a change? Compared to the last few days, she looked downright chipper.

Only now did Penny notice that her client was wearing an anorak and a thick woolen scarf to go with it.

"Get your jacket, I have to show you something," Miriam exclaimed.

Penny still felt a little dazed from her unplanned siesta. "Did something happen?" she asked as she turned to the hook where her coat hung.

"I remember now how I know the symbol you photographed," Miriam said, beaming from ear to ear. "The little flame from Grandma's diaries!"

Penny perked up. "Seriously? Where from?"

"Come on, come with me, I'll show you. I just discovered it by chance. Although I must have had it in front of my eyes a hundred times. Just never paid attention to it. But today I noticed it because you showed me the photo!"

"Where did you find it?" asked Penny, already slipping into her coat.

"At the cemetery. At grandmother's grave. The family grave."

"That's where you saw the flame?"

Miriam nodded vigorously. "I've just been there. And I'm quite sure it's the same symbol. Come on. It must mean something, right? Grandma must have been trying to tell me something with it!"

No doubt she wanted to, Penny thought. The only question was: what?

"Why have you been at your grandmother's grave?" she asked Miriam as they left the room together and walked down the stairs. "Do you go there often?"

Miriam did not answer right away. At first, she made a face as if she didn't quite know what to say, then she suddenly stopped in the middle of the stairs. She looked around, probably to make sure they were alone, then leaned over to Penny and whispered, "I was hoping Grandma might show herself to me. Give me a sign that she's still alive, you know? Now that you've seen her. After all, she knows I visit her grave often. And the cemetery is a very lonely place. You won't get disturbed there at all, if you meet in secret."

Penny groaned inwardly. She had thought too little about this kind of consequence when she had told her tall tale to the hotel residents. When she had claimed so grandiosely that she had seen the dead Johanna Lempra with her own eyes. Alive.

It was obvious that Miriam hoped to be reunited with her grandmother soon. That she assumed everything would be like before, once the murderer was caught. Or to put it more precisely: the assassin. If it was claimed that Johanna had actually survived his attack, then he was no longer a murderer. With such a brazen lie, it was already difficult to use the right vocabulary ...

In any case, Miriam was in for a painful disappointment. That was inevitable. Surely it would feel to her as if she were losing her beloved grandmother for a second time when she learned the truth in the end.

Was it worth it? Penny could only hope so. Because whether the lie would actually lead her to Johanna's killer was still doubtful.

She started moving again, taking the last steps of the stairs, and turning over her shoulder to Miriam. "Come on, let's go. I want to be back before it gets dark." Even if she didn't feel immediately threatened by the killer, she certainly wasn't comfortable with the idea of wandering around a deserted, half-ruined cemetery in the falling dusk.

Arriving at the cemetery, Miriam walked straight to the grave where the lush bouquet of red roses that Wilhelm had placed there yesterday still lay.

She paid no attention to the flowers, however, but directed Penny's attention to one of the two grave lanterns that were symmetrically placed to the left and right of the marble angel.

They were wrought-iron lanterns, fitted at their lower end into the stone of the grave border. Miriam pointed excitedly to the left of the two lanterns. "Look, Penny!"

Penny crouched down—and immediately realized that Miriam was right. The milky glass panes of the grave lamp were decorated with the symbol she had discovered in Johanna's diaries. Small flames were carved on all four sides.

"I always thought they were just ornaments," Miriam said, shaking her head. "I mean, flames on a lantern—that's nothing unusual. That's why I never really paid attention."

Penny agreed with her. Carefully, she opened the door of the small lantern. Inside, a grave candle flickered, almost burned all the way down.

Hm, it seemed to be just a regular cemetery lantern, like a thousand others.

What was this all about? Why had Johanna led them here?

Learn from the past—the words from the strange letter the old lady had left her granddaughter suddenly came back to Penny's mind. They had to refer to studying the diaries. By reading the accounts her grandmother had written down over the decades, Miriam could learn from the past. Learn something about her grandmother's life and work.

The old lady had probably expected her granddaughter to read these texts at some point, even though Miriam had shown little interest in detective work. Besides, Johanna must have speculated that Miriam would regularly visit her grave—where she could recognize the flames on the lanterns.

The old master detective had been wrong with one of these two assumptions—the former—even though she might have been almost infallible in the hunt for murderers. Well, one's own family members often proved the most difficult people to figure out. Penny herself knew that only too well.

She carefully pulled the grave candle out of its case and set it down beside her. The small light went out on the spot in the icy wind that whistled around the graves.

Not a pretty symbolism, it went through Penny's mind, but that couldn't be helped now. Still, she couldn't fight off a sudden chill, warm as her winter coat might have been.

She knelt directly in front of the lantern, peered inside, and scanned the interior with her right hand. The grave candle had been standing on a metal plate that was fastened to the bottom of the case with four screws.

Penny tapped the plate with a fingernail—and was rewarded with the sound she had hoped for.

"Doesn't sound solid, does it?" she said to Miriam. There had to be a cavity under the metal plate—even if it couldn't be very large. On the outside, the base of the lantern was barely five centimeters high.

She needed a screwdriver, but that was unfortunately

not one of the standard utensils a woman usually carried around in her handbag. Not even if the woman was a budding detective.

It was Miriam who unexpectedly handed her a pocket knife. One of those Swiss souvenirs that, in addition to several blades, also concealed a tiny file, scissors and even a toothpick inside.

Miriam acknowledged Penny's surprised look with a shrug. "Theo gave it to me once. I carry it with me almost all the time."

The tip of the file just fit into the narrow slots of the four screw heads. Penny hastily set to work.

She almost squealed with excitement when a narrow package wrapped in plastic emerged from under the metal plate. A padded envelope, as it turned out, after Penny had removed the protective foil.

It had already been neatly slit open with a knife. Johanna Lempra's name and address were written on the front, along with the annotations:

Private.
By messenger.

The sender's data was printed on the back in the form of a seal:

David Blüthenstein
New York City

Nothing else, no complete mailing address.

Penny handed Miriam the envelope. "You should take a look at this," she said, "Your grandmother wanted you to find it."

Miriam accepted the envelope, peered inside first, and then carefully pulled out a single sheet of stationery.

She read silently, her eyes wide and her lips slightly parted. Finally, she handed the paper back to Penny.

"I don't understand this ..."

Penny looked at the letter. It had a date on it that was over eight years ago.

Dear Johanna,

You will be surprised to hear from me because we have never met in person. My name is David Blüthenstein, and I owe my life to your grandfather.

In the next two paragraphs followed the life story of David Blüthenstein—summarized in just a few lines.

Youth and an early career in his parents' jewelry business in Vienna between the wars, then the sudden arrest of his parents by Nazi henchmen in 1941. David fled with his young wife to Mönchswald, to the Grandhotel then run by Johanna's grandfather Matthias. The Blüthensteins had often spent their summer vacations there in better days.

He could not put into words his gratitude, David wrote further, for Matthias keeping him and his wife hidden from the Nazis for several months, putting his own life at risk.

Finally, the young couple managed to escape from Austria in a daring cloak-and-dagger operation; first to Switzerland and then to the USA. In America David again became active as a jeweler and had apparently been very successful.

Penny continued to read:

God was good to us, giving us a new life in America, even though we missed our old home forever. However, we were not blessed with children of our own; so now that my wife is already with our Creator, and my time on earth is also coming to an end, I will bestow most of my fortune upon a charitable foundation for victims of the Holocaust.

However, to you, my dear Johanna, as a descendant of our savior, I would like to leave a few particularly rare stones from my private collection. Because your grandfather was an equally rare and precious specimen of the human species. May they give you happiness and joy.

God bless you,
David Blüthenstein.

"What kind of stones?" Miriam wanted to know when Penny had finished reading the letter. "What is this man talking about? And who is he anyway?"

"Didn't your grandmother ever tell you that story? About the Jewish couple her own grandfather hid in the Grandhotel?"

Miriam frowned and nibbled on her index finger. She

seemed to be pondering. "Yes, I think she mentioned it once ... It was ages ago, when I was a teenager at most. But I'm afraid I wasn't really listening. I find war stories even creepier than murders."

"I see," Penny murmured as she moved a few puzzle pieces into place in her mind. David's letter proved irrevocably that Johanna's grandfather had not been a Nazi sympathizer or even a murderer. Matthias had not killed the Blüthensteins to get his hands on their diamonds. Which meant that there was no treasure to be found in the Grandhotel. Unless ...

"What about these stones this David mentions?" Miriam interrupted her train of thought. "If he was a jeweler, is he talking about precious stones?"

Penny nodded. "About diamonds, possibly."

"Diamonds?" Miriam's eyes widened. "But where are they?" She peeked into the envelope again, but it contained nothing but the single sheet of paper.

"That's a really good question," Penny replied. "David Blüthenstein had the letter delivered by messenger, and the envelope is padded. You don't do that when you're just delivering a letter. I guess he must have enclosed the gems."

"Sounds logical," Miriam said, looking at her expectantly.

Up to this point, the puzzle Johanna had set her granddaughter had been fairly easy to crack. If Miriam had read her grandmother's diaries even superficially, she would have found the clues leading to David Blüthenstein's letter—even without Penny's help.

Learn from the past. These words Johanna left her granddaughter had a double meaning; Penny now realized. They related to Johanna's own past in the form of the diaries, but also to the story of Miriam's great-great-grandfather Matthias, who had been a hero and saved the lives of the Blüthensteins.

But what now? Where was the gift that Johanna had promised her granddaughter? *Learn from the past, and you will never be a beggar again.*

Surely this had to refer to the diamonds David Blüthenstein had given Johanna as a gift. After all, the clue of the flame symbols had led directly to his letter. To this package, which had clearly contained more than just a sheet of paper. And the symbols in the diaries did not go back further than eight years. Johanna must have started to lay this trail shortly after David Blüthenstein had written to her.

You're missing something essential here, Penny, she told herself.

Only what? She studied the letter again, which she still held in her hand. But there were no further clues on this sheet, that much was obvious.

Presumably it would be possible to contact David Blüthenstein in New York and ask him what exactly he had sent Johanna.

Wait, no, he had written that his life was about to end—and that had been eight years ago. And he had left no children. No one who could provide any information now ...

Was finding the letter here in the cemetery only the

first stage of Johanna's puzzle? A relatively simple task, just to warm up? Was the second step a real challenge to a detective's skills? Did the old master sleuth want to put Miriam's talents to the test before she gave her the diamonds?

If that was the case, it didn't reflect well on Penny. She imagined that she had what it took to be a detective—and yet she was completely in the dark about what to do next.

Or was the riddle possibly no longer valid? Johanna had already thought it up eight years ago—shortly after David Blüthenstein had bequeathed her the diamonds. This was proven by the flame symbols in her diaries.

Had Miriam's grandmother sold the gems at some point because the Grandhotel was running out of money? Had she merely not had the chance to erase the trail in the old diaries and remove David's letter from the cemetery lantern before her unexpected death?

So many questions—they'd almost made Penny forget that she also had to solve a murder case.

When she dropped onto her bed hours later with her head spinning, she slept even worse than the night before.

Nevertheless—or precisely because of this?—she had come up with a foolhardy plan the next morning.

20

Tuesday, February 12

Early on Tuesday morning, Penny set out to find Jakub. She didn't know where exactly his third-floor quarters were located, but she was sure he was already scurrying around the house again somewhere. Or snooping. Probably both.

She found his cleaning cart in front of the room that Armin occupied. The door was ajar, and a vacuum cleaner could be heard from inside. Penny was not shy about entering unbidden.

Jakub flinched when she appeared in front of him. His look was guilty—but to all appearances he had only been cleaning. He hadn't rummaged through any drawers or anything like that.

"Miss Küfer," he croaked. "Mr. Keyser has already gone out."

Penny nodded. "It doesn't matter. I was coming to see you anyway."

Was Armin already on the treasure hunt again? Was he still scouring the labyrinthine old building in search of the diamonds? If so, he was wasting his time. Penny knew by now that the Blüthensteins and their gems had made it safe and sound to America.

Unless ...

A new thought crept into her head. What if the diamonds were hidden somewhere in the hotel after all? Not since the Nazi-era, but for the last eight years, since Johanna had received the small package from David Blüthenstein?

Miriam's grandmother might have hidden the gems somewhere in the building—as the second part of the task she had set her granddaughter. Because she wanted Miriam to be a sleuth as well.

Had Armin been on the trail of *these* diamonds? Had he wanted to get his hands on the jewels and murdered Johanna for it?

Then what am I doing here with Jakub? Penny asked herself. Was she barking up the wrong tree? Did she have it all backwards after all?

No, she had to be right, because Armin ...

She didn't get any further, because Jakub's shrill voice snapped her out of her thoughts.

"What can I do for you, Miss Küfer?" he asked, stepping closer to her. Too close for her taste.

She took a step back. Armed with his vacuum cleaner, the janitor looked like a modern Don Quixote, comical but also somehow tragic. Surely, he performed legendary heroic deeds in his dreams instead of vacuuming the floors in a run-down hotel.

"It's about Johanna," she began—just as she had prepared beforehand. For once, she didn't have to improvise.

The words had the desired effect. Jakub straightened

his shoulders and gripped his vacuum cleaner even tighter. Determined to do anything.

"Have you seen her again?" he asked eagerly. "Talked to her?"

"She has slipped me a message," Penny said, emphasizing each word as if she were exchanging highly sensitive information with a secret agent.

"Oh! And what was it about, if you don't mind me asking?"

"She requested my help," Penny replied. "I was right about my theory, you see. Irmi *was* collaborating with her. The two of them devised a plan to trap the killer. Or rather, the attacker, since he did fail to kill Johanna."

"But he has Irmi on his conscience!" interrupted Jakub, "She *is* dead!"

"I know. This criminal is a particularly cunning and unscrupulous person. We have to proceed very carefully."

"We?" The janitor raised his eyebrows and ran his tongue over his chapped lips.

"Yes, as I said, I need your help. I want you to be my life insurance."

Jakub nodded eagerly. "Sure. Of course. I'd love to. What do you have in mind?"

Penny tried hard to make her voice sound even more conspiratorial.

"So, here's what happened with Irmi—this much I know by now: Johanna haunted the house to scare the killer. He was supposed to think that she was stalking him from beyond the grave. Hunting him down, you know. Or that she had survived his attack, and that he now had to silence her at all costs before she could expose him."

"Um, which is it?" asked Jakub. "Was she trying to pass herself off as a ghost, or make the killer realize that he had failed to murder her?"

"Both, I suspect. After all, she didn't know who had attacked her at first. As you remember, she was pushed down the stairs. She didn't get to see the assassin. And so, I guess, for the, um, devout hotel residents, like yourself, she chose to play the role of the restless soul, while others were supposed to think she was a flesh-and-blood human being."

"She can't have really assumed that I wanted to murder her!" exclaimed Jakub.

Penny smiled apologetically and said in a sugary voice, "Clearly a miscalculation. No idea, how she could possibly suspect you. Well, anyway, Johanna is an old lady and not so mobile anymore. That's how she came up with the idea of making Irmi her accomplice, whom she probably trusted unconditionally –"

"The insolence!" Jakub worked himself up, "I was at least as devoted to her as this ..." He couldn't think of the right word for the cook. He croaked something unintelligible, and at the same time his pointed nose twitched excitedly.

"I saw that right away," Penny lied. "That you are one hundred percent trustworthy, I mean. That's exactly why I'm turning to you now. And you can also convince Johanna by helping me."

Jakub growled something that was probably meant to

express agreement.

"Well," Penny continued, "Johanna made Irmi her ally, and the cook then occasionally impersonated the old lady. Especially when it came to invading bedrooms and then disappearing again like a ghost. Climbing balconies just wasn't Johanna's thing anymore. While Irmi was very athletic."

"Well," Jakub grumbled and looked a bit more conciliatory. He probably just realized that he would have felt little desire to risk dangerous climbs for his boss. Loyalty or not.

"Irmi then also took on the role of Johanna in the trap they set for the killer. Where exactly she lured him and how she did it—I don't know yet. But it doesn't matter. In any case, Irmi took this opportunity to equip herself with a buttonhole camera or something similar. You know, those barely visible thingies that can nevertheless make great recordings."

Jakub nodded eagerly. "Yes, yes, of course."

Penny continued, "Before Irmi fell off the balcony, she must have managed to confront the killer and get him to confess. Or at least to make some compromising statements. Or maybe it was just that he wanted to get at her because he actually thought she was Johanna. In any case, her mini-camera recorded usable evidence. Then, when Irmi fell to her death—or was pushed—Johanna managed to get the device off her. She had been lying in wait down in the parking lot. Or at the edge of the forest just behind it. You remember, I saw her disappear between the trees. She fled with the evidence Irmi's camera had recorded. This much she wrote to me in the message she sent me."

"Ohhh," Jakub said, "so she has proof?"

"Exactly. And since I saw her when I found Irmi's body, she must have noticed me as well, of course. Maybe she already knew why I'm at the hotel. I'm sure Irmi told her all about me. And that's why she's now asked *me* for help. I found this under my door this morning."

She unfolded a letter written in Johanna Lempra's neat handwriting and shoved it right under Jakub's nose.

"I guess that with Irmi's video recording she has irrefutable evidence against the murderer in hand. She will probably want to hand over this video to me so that I can pass it on to the authorities. She hasn't told me her exact plan, as you can see."

She pointed to the letter, which Jakub studied with narrowed eyes.

"I don't think Johanna wants to give up her cover just yet," she continued. "As long as she's officially presumed dead, she's safest."

"You're supposed to meet her at the cemetery?" Jakub read from the letter.

"Yes, tonight, in the old cottage—I don't know what it may have once been. A rectory?"

Jakub shook his head. "The cemetery keeper's house, but that was many years ago."

"OK. Anyway, it's the perfect meeting point. Remote, lonely, forgotten by the world ... just the place if you don't want to be seen."

"Yes," Jakub said with a sparkle in his eye. "And now

you want me to protect you, don't you? "

Penny suppressed a smile and shook her head. "A truly honorable offer, Jakub, but it would be far too dangerous. Just think of Irmi."

"I'm not afraid," the janitor declared. He straightened to his full height, looking more like a ruffled songbird than ever. "Of no one!"

"I know you're not," Penny said. "But I need you here. You're my life insurance. Johanna will be proud of you!"

"But, I—"

"Listen to my plan," Penny interrupted him. "I want to go to the meeting with Johanna. But I need someone to watch my back. You keep an eye on the hotel and call me the minute anyone leaves after me. Would you do that? I don't want to lead the killer straight to Johanna. Nor necessarily risk my own neck."

"You are quite a brave lady," Jakub said admiringly.

"Not really," Penny replied. "I'm getting sick just thinking about going to that cemetery alone at night."

That wasn't even a lie. "But it has to be done. It's the one chance to finally bring the killer to justice. If I'm not back after two hours at the latest, you call the police, OK? No matter which story you have to tell them, they have to come to the cemetery!"

"Yes, all right, Miss Küfer. You can count on Jakub!"

"I knew that," Penny said, giving the birdman a smile.

He cleared his throat, then hesitated for a moment. He seemed to have something else on his mind.

Finally, he lowered his voice and asked, "Do you already have a suspicion, Miss Küfer? Who the murderer might be? Johanna didn't tell you, did she?"

Penny pretended to hesitate, then said, "I'm afraid I don't have a clue; I'm completely in the dark. I need Johanna's help to close this case. Keep your fingers crossed that everything goes according to plan tonight."

21

After leaving Jakub to his work again, Penny ran down the stairs and headed for the breakfast room.

Actually, breakfast time was already over, but she was lucky. One table was still occupied, exactly by the man she was looking for: Wilhelm Lindner.

He had made himself comfortable with a cup of coffee and was reading the morning paper. Miriam, on the other hand, was nowhere to be seen; she had probably already turned to her other tasks at the hotel and left Wilhelm to his own devices.

"May I join you?" asked Penny.

"Certainly." The old man looked up from his newspaper only briefly, then he wanted to continue to devote himself to the article he was reading.

"Johanna Lempra sent me a message—and I wanted to ask for your help," Penny blurted out.

The announcement achieved the desired effect. Wilhelm raised his head, looked at her in amazement, and the very next moment he folded up his newspaper.

She pulled the letter out of her purse that she had already shown to the janitor and described her nightly plan to Wilhelm. In doing so, she chose almost the same words as she had used earlier with Jakub.

"But I'll need your support if it's going to work," she

ended. "I'll need someone to watch my back. And to call the police if I don't come back."

"You really want to go to this meeting?", Wilhelm asked. "It's much too dangerous, isn't it? It could be a trap!"

"I don't think so. The letter is in Johanna's handwriting, isn't it? I recognize it from her diaries. And she certainly knows what she's doing. She's a professional. She faked her own death, can you imagine! Like Sherlock Holmes himself! I trust her. And for my part, I'll make sure she doesn't actually die in the end."

Wilhelm nodded slowly. "I am honored that you put your trust in me. That you're asking me for help."

Penny looked him straight in the eye. "You and Johanna—that was more than just a friendship, wasn't it? You loved her. Or rather, you still do. I saw you at the cemetery. With the bouquet of roses. Forgive me for being so blunt, but the expression on your face when you knelt by Johanna's grave and communed with her in your thoughts –"

"You've been watching me?"

"I'm sorry," Penny said. "It wasn't intentional."

Which wasn't entirely true, but Wilhelm didn't need to know that. "Anyway, I've rarely seen a person who grieved so deeply. Who felt so much for the woman he loved. Am I not right? Don't worry, your secret is safe with me."

Wilhelm lowered his head, staring at his hands, which were disfigured by gout.

"My secret," he murmured. "You are a good detective,

Miss Küfer. You're right. I love Johanna—have loved her all my life."

"What went wrong?" asked Penny in a gentle tone. "Why didn't you two become a couple? Judging from what Johanna writes in her diaries, she's just as devoted to you. More than friendly, too, I think."

Wilhelm raised his head. His eyelids twitched.

"I ruined it," he said. "Our love. The life we could have had. It's all my fault. I let myself be blinded. By Sabine. Or rather, by her parents' money. By the splendid house they lived in. I know how that must sound for someone of your generation, Miss Küfer, but back then ..."

He blinked his eyes. Ran his fingers first over his beard, then through his thick white hair. As if that were a way to brush off unpleasant memories.

"My own family was poor," he said then. "And I mean really poor. There's nothing like that in Austria today, thank God. Johanna and I ... we loved each other, but I had nothing to offer her. One didn't marry simply for love in those days. That was not enough. As a man, you had to be able to provide for your wife. Give her a good life. I wasn't able to do that. And instead of standing my ground and making something of myself, I chickened out. I took the easy way out and married Sabine, who had taken a fancy to me. I got into her parents' jewelry store. Worked there until I retired. But I swear to you, not a day went by that I didn't regret my decision."

"And you couldn't get a divorce?" Penny asked. "Because they just didn't do that back then?"

"Oh, I would have defied convention, eventually. I was

so unhappy in my marriage that in the end I didn't care about anything. But Johanna had also married in the meantime. It was too late. All we had left was friendship. It wasn't until I had to commit my wife to a nursing home because she was completely lost in her dementia, and Johanna's husband died –"

He interrupted himself, drying the single tear that had rolled down his cheek with his shirt sleeve.

"Only then did I dare to think of a late happiness. I moved here to the hotel, took residence as a permanent guest—and tried to get closer to Johanna again. Gently, you understand? At our age, a romantic new beginning is an almost ridiculous undertaking. But I do think we would have become a couple if she hadn't ... oh, you know."

"If she hadn't been murdered?"

He nodded silently. Then he composed himself and looked Penny in the eye. "And now you're claiming she's still alive!" He shook his head in disbelief. "You can count on me tonight. I'll phone you if anyone should be following you. And if you don't return in time, I'll alert the police. Though I would like nothing more than to accompany you. If only I could see Johanna again!"

22

Shortly after 10 p.m., Penny left the Grandhotel and made her way to the cemetery.

The night was bitter cold and so dark that she could barely see a few meters ahead. Still, she resisted the temptation to use her cell phone flashlight or to peer over her own shoulder every few steps to see if she was being followed. One was allowed to be a little afraid, as a woman alone, at night in this remote area. But she couldn't afford to give the killer any idea that she was expecting him.

Which of the two men would come after her to finish her off? And Johanna too, who had supposedly escaped death. Two birds with one stone. Or rather, two annoying snoopers with one stone. Hopefully, the murderer would not be able to resist this offer.

She still didn't know who she would have to deal with. Jakub or Wilhelm? One of these two had murdered Johanna Lempra, of that she was 99% sure.

She had been able to narrow down her list of suspects this far, but two possible murderers was one too many. Apart from the fact that she didn't have a shred of evidence. So the trap at the cemetery was her only chance.

She zipped her anorak up to under her nose and wrapped her scarf tighter. God, it was cold out here. And dark. She wanted to turn around right then and there.

A detective knows no fear, she reminded herself. Every few steps she repeated the sentence, like a mantra. It sounded childish, almost ridiculous. Like something out of a B-movie on TV, but still it helped. At least a little bit.

When she reached the cemetery, she climbed effortlessly over the half-ruined outer wall and headed for the former cottage of the cemetery keeper. It had already looked creepy during the day, but now ...

She swallowed. Just keep walking, Penny. One foot in front of the other. And stop looking around all the time!

Carefully, she pulled open the door, which hung emaciated on its hinges. There was no lock, and what would have been the point? There had been nothing to steal here for a long time.

Not a nice place to die, it went through her mind.

Oh gosh, Penny, please don't be so melodramatic! Everything will be all right ...

She closed the door behind her as tightly as she managed to and turned on her cell phone light. She also checked to see if she had phone reception in here. Yes ... good.

She fingered—probably for the hundredth time in the last ten minutes—the bulge in her jacket pocket. Her gas pistol with pepper ammunition. She had bought this weapon only a week ago. Every adult in Austria could legally carry such a thing, even without a gun license.

In her training at the Argus Academy, Penny had learned how extremely effective pepper bullets could be. You couldn't kill anyone with them—which she didn't intend to do anyway—but the gas irritated the eyes, nasal mucosa and respiratory tract to the extreme. Thereby, an opponent could be knocked out for a good half hour. At least that's what the instructor had claimed. Penny fervently hoped that she would not have to test the weapon in practice tonight.

Now it was just a matter of laying in ambush and waiting. Being patient. She retreated to a corner of the room where there was the least amount of debris and turned off her cell phone light.

She couldn't have told how much time passed. It felt like hours, but it was probably no more than ten minutes.

A barely perceptible squeak of the door hinges and a ray of moonlight suddenly falling into the room betrayed the arrival of the killer.

With a swift movement, Penny turned her cell phone back on, took a few steps forward and pointed the light at the newcomer—along with the barrel of her gas pistol.

"Don't move," she said. Or rather, she croaked it, because her mouth felt terribly dry, and she found she could barely control her vocal cords. Apart from the fact that "Don't move!" sounded downright ridiculous, like a TV thriller. But she couldn't think of a more eloquent phrase. Damn it, that really didn't matter now!

In the cone of light of her cell phone stood—Jakub! He was wrapped up to his nose in a dingy fur jacket, holding a blade that looked like a kitchen knife.

So the trap had been sprung, just as Penny had

planned! The janitor had followed her instead of waiting for her at the hotel as promised. He had come to finish her and Johanna Lempra off.

She held him in check with her gun. Now she just had to make him talk so that the tiny microphone she had hidden under the collar of her anorak could record something. His confession!

Jakub, however, stood there completely motionless—looking scared to death.

"Miss Küfer," he stammered, staring straight down the barrel of her pistol. "What are you doing? It's only me, right. I was worried about you! Where is Mrs. Lempra?"

"You were worried? And the knife in your hand?"

"I didn't come here defenseless! I thought you might need a protector."

He looked so tiny and helpless in his shaggy jacket that Penny almost felt the need to protect *him*. But she couldn't be fooled, this man had dozens of people on his conscience!

"If you are telling the truth, and the knife is really only for defense, then you can put it away now, can't you? As you can see, no one is in danger here."

Jakub looked around, hesitated for a moment. "Yes, well," he then said, bending down and putting the blade on the floor.

"Where is Mrs. Lempra?" he asked again as he straightened up.

Something was not right here. Was the janitor such a good actor? Was he just trying to lull her into a sense of security? She eyed him over the barrel of her gas pistol, which she clutched so tightly that her wrists ached. But Jakub just stood there calmly and seemed to be waiting for something to happen.

The only way was *in medias res*, Penny decided. Get right to the point, accuse him of murder. Her palms, clutching the gun, felt sweaty, despite the freezing cold in the old building.

"I know you killed Johanna," she began.

A rather clumsy opening, but she couldn't think of anything better just now. Oh Lord, what kind of detective was she? That was the kind of stuff you prepared in advance, so that you'd damn well have the right words ready when the time came!

"What, me?" squeaked the janitor. He puffed up to his full height. "How can you say such a thing, Miss Küfer! You know perfectly well that –"

"Jakub is innocent," a man's voice suddenly cut through the darkness. A voice behind Penny's back—one she recognized even before she whirled around.

Wilhelm Lindner.

She was too slow.

"Drop the gun," he ordered before she had even brought him into focus. He himself was holding a pistol that was clearly not a gas weapon.

Looks like a Beretta, she thought.

Great, now was exactly the right time for gun identification exercises.

"Drop it, Miss Küfer," Wilhelm repeated in an emphatically calm voice. He still spoke like the nice older gentleman she had met in the hotel—but there was a

determination in his eyes that was new to her. A determination she would never have believed this quiet,
friendly man could have in him.

She cursed herself under her breath. The element of
surprise was on his side. Instead of on hers, as she had
planned. She had been so focused on Jakub for the last
few minutes that she had blocked out everything else
around her. There must have been sounds as Wilhelm
had crept up on her. An old man was no panther, after
all. And how had he gotten in anyway? Did this dilapidated house have a back entrance? Had Wilhelm been
here all along, lying in wait?

Anyway, she stood no chance against him. Even if they
both fired their weapons at the same time. He would
make painful acquaintance with a cloud of pepper gas—
but she would bite the dust. Damn it.

As if in slow motion, she got down on her knees and
put her gun on the ground.

"Good girl," Wilhelm commented.

Jakub stared at him in disbelief. "What are you doing,
Mr. Lindner?" he asked. Apparently, he was slow on the
uptake.

Wilhelm ignored him.

"Not bad," he said to Penny instead. "You lured us both
here, Jakub and me? The two of us made it onto your
shortlist? Not a bad idea at all, I must say. You're a bright
young woman. But you shouldn't overestimate yourself.
Other people aren't stupid either. To be more specific:
I'm certainly not. Do you really think I didn't realize you
were trying to trap me?"

Penny said nothing. She thought feverishly about what she could possibly do now. How could she escape this situation she had maneuvered herself into with her skin intact? She needed inspiration. And quickly.

"You did a good job of forging Johanna's handwriting," Wilhelm said. "In that letter you tried to lure me with. The one she supposedly wrote to you. You have creative talent, and in Johanna's archive there was enough text material available to you as a sample. But I *know* Johanna's handwriting. We've been writing letters to each other all our lives."

He fell silent, paused for a moment, and seemed to be lost in thought. "You couldn't fool me," he then said. "With that silly story that Irmi secretly recorded a video confession from the killer—which Johanna then took possession of."

He shook his head. "Johanna is dead."

His voice was suddenly husky, no longer as confident as it had been a moment ago. "I have personally convinced myself of that fact, at the foot of the stairs, that unspeakable night. Even if I didn't want her to die. Nor do I want to kill you, by the way, Miss Küfer, even if you must forgive me for finding it much easier this time. I loved Johanna. You, on the other hand, are just a stranger who is too curious for her own good."

"I hear that a lot," Penny grumbled. Still her thoughts rattled, spinning in circles. *A way out! Right now!* Damn it, there was nothing but emptiness in her head. She was so screwed.

"I thought I'd take the opportunity tonight anyway,

trap or no trap," Wilhelm said. "After all, you left me no choice. What would you have done if I hadn't shown up here? You probably would have gone to the police in the end. Even if they're not exactly interested in the theories of amateur sleuths. You're not the type to take no for an answer, Miss Küfer. At least, that's my assessment of you."

"You're damn right about that," Penny said.

"Miriam came to me with the clever little observation you made in Johanna's diaries. Just last night. She told me everything. You really upset the poor child by accusing Johanna of being a vigilante! And that was a little too close to the truth for me. You will surely understand that. Thus, unfortunately, you have forced me to act."

"I quickly realized it wasn't Johanna doing vigilante justice, believe me," Penny said.

"Possibly, yes. And then, of course, I was the next best candidate, right? Or our esteemed janitor."

He cast a sidelong glance at Jakub, who stood rigid as a pillar of salt beside them. "I guess it wasn't very hard for you to narrow down the circle of suspects to just the two of us, huh? I hope you don't think it's a brilliant feat of detective work. I mean, there weren't many possibilities. Irmi is dead, and Mr. Keyser, our dashing adventurer, hasn't lived in the hotel long enough. It couldn't have been him, who had been providing justice for years, among the criminal scum Johanna exposed. The same goes for Christiane Wittmann, who seemed so promising to you at first, didn't she? Both just guests of the recent past."

"That's true," Penny said. "It didn't take a stroke of genius to come up with Jakub or yourself as the only possible culprits in the end. And it's also true that I would have gone to the police if you hadn't shown up tonight. Believe me, I would have managed to make them listen to me. I can be quite persistent when it comes down to it. The death rate among the murderers Johanna exposed is far too high to believe in coincidence. Or in divine justice. I don't know why Johanna herself didn't notice this much sooner."

"She was a very devout person," Wilhelm said. "And constantly surrounded by death. But in the end, of course, she did notice ..."

"That's what I thought," Penny said. "That's why she had to die ... But even if you commit two more murders now, you won't get away with it, Mr. Lindner! This time it won't pass as an accident. An investigation will be launched, and the police will certainly take a closer look at Johanna's diaries. Miriam now knows about the vigilante issue. She won't keep quiet about it if something happens to me tonight."

"Possible," Wilhelm said. He sounded tired and resigned. "But I guess I'll have to risk it. Surely you can see that. I can't just let you go, I'm honestly sorry."

Penny almost believed him. He seemed genuinely distressed. He didn't murder out for pleasure, but out of necessity. At least from his perspective. But that didn't help her in the least.

Wilhelm raised the barrel of his pistol. "I guess that's it," he said. "We've discussed everything, haven't we? I'll refrain from giving you a long, drawn-out explanation now of why I did what I had to do—while you figure out an escape plan. I am accountable to no one. Not even Johanna, whom I adored, wanted to understand me. "

"You're accountable to *me*," said a woman's voice behind them.

23

Penny whirled around. A small cry escaped the janitor, who had been frozen in fear.

It was Miriam who came down the dilapidated staircase from the second floor behind them. In her hand, she held a revolver that looked as if it had already witnessed the Second World War.

The safest place is in front of the gun. These words of the instructor at the shooting range had actually been meant for Penny—but as wildly as Miriam's hands were shaking now, her aim was certainly no better. In the end, she would shoot one of them, completely unintentionally. If the half-rotten staircase didn't collapse under her weight first.

"What the hell are you doing here?" Penny hissed at her young client.

Miriam struggled to stabilize the gun in her hands. "I wanted to stand by Grandmother," she cried defiantly. "And you! I didn't want to be a coward for once in my life! I overheard you, you and him here—" She gave Wilhelm a snide look. Apparently, it had escaped her notice that he now pointed his pistol at her, and that his hands, unlike hers, were not trembling a bit.

"Overheard?" he asked in surprise.

"During your conversation in the breakfast room this morning! You probably thought you were undisturbed—but I was in the kitchen. And the door was just ajar. I kept quiet when I realized what you were talking about."

Penny groaned inwardly. Again, she had made a cardinal mistake. She should have made sure that she and Wilhelm were really alone! Now she had dragged Miriam into the matter as well—and would probably have her client on her conscience within the next five minutes. Because now Wilhelm had to kill her, too, if he wanted to get away with his crimes.

"Is that Johanna's revolver?" he asked her. "Drop it, Miriam, you can't even handle it!"

"Yes, I can," she countered. Her voice was barely more than a whisper, but she jutted out her chin determinedly. "And unlike Grandma, I even have a gun license. Ask Penny!"

Penny nodded vigorously. Although she had no illusions about who would win any shooting duel between Miriam and Wilhelm. If Miriam really had the courage to pull the trigger, she would at most shoot herself in the foot. Or finish off Penny or Jakub.

"No wonder Grandmother turned to you with her letter, Penny," Miriam said. "That she asked you to help her. Instead of me, her own granddaughter! She knows what a coward I am! But where is she, anyway? She's not really dead like Willi just claimed, is she?" She gave Penny a pleading look.

"Yes, she is," Wilhelm said before Penny could utter a word. "Miss Küfer lied, she just made up the whole story to trap me."

"That's not true!" cried Miriam. She staggered down the last flight of stairs as if Wilhelm had hit her. "Tell me it's not true, Penny!"

Penny said nothing in reply. Now was really not the time for lengthy explanations. The lie about Johanna Lempra's survival had served its purpose. The murderer had fallen into her trap. Except that he would probably be the only one to leave the old cemetery keeper's house alive.

At that moment, she registered that Miriam's revolver didn't even have the hammer cocked. Which meant that Miriam would have to apply enormous pressure with her finger on the trigger if she wanted to fire the gun in this condition. What did the instructor say again? 8.5 kilograms of pressure required for the average revolver?

Penny had not possessed that strength, in target practice. Her client, on the other hand, who had been a waitress for many years, hopefully had more powerful hand muscles. But Penny doubted anyway that she would actually pull the trigger.

Miriam was wearing that bracelet again, the one she had worn to weapons class. The colorful stones, the plastic beads that looked like bubble gum balls, and the silver owls and dolphins danced and swayed on the chain because Miriam's hand was shaking so badly. Even worse than back then in class.

Back then ... It was only a few days ago.

At that moment, a thought exploded in Penny's adrenaline-flooded brain. One that didn't help her in the least in the hopeless situation she was in at the moment. Indeed one that didn't even have anything to do with the murder of Johanna Lempra.

Miriam's mysterious inheritance! That's what it was all about.

You will never be a beggar again. Johanna had promised this in her letter to her granddaughter. If Miriam learned from the past, as the old master sleuth had put it.

The solution to the riddle Johanna had posed to her granddaughter was cunning, ingeniously simple, and at the same time completely insane. Penny saw it so clearly before her eyes as if a movie screen had stretched across the gloom of the old cottage. In 3D and IMAX format.

Except that Miriam would never get to enjoy her inheritance unless a miracle happened within the next few minutes.

Wilhelm still had his pistol pointed at Miriam. The two faced each other a few meters apart and looked into each other's eyes. Like two duelists. Wilhelm's hand on the trigger was perfectly still, but there was no longer that grim determination in his face that he had displayed earlier. Before Miriam had shown up.

"Drop the gun, child," he repeated. There was genuine concern in his voice. Genuine affection. "I don't want to lose you, too."

Miriam did not move from the spot. Her eyes reflected a mixture of disappointment, hatred, and fear.

Penny and Jakub stood by absolutely defenseless. As if they were only uninvolved spectators. But they weren't. *We're all going to die here if you don't think of something right now, Penny! Come on, think!*

Feverishly, she searched her memory for insights from the detective course that could save her life here and now.

But nothing came up. The situation she had gotten herself into—along with her client!—was simply not on the syllabus.

"Professional detectives don't solve murder cases like in TV crime shows," their instructor had assured them at the beginning of the course. "The most dangerous thing you'll encounter in your career is a wife you have to inform that her husband is cheating on her."

My ass. The curriculum was in desperate need of an update!

But suddenly, something did pop up in Penny's overheated brain. It was just a single sentence that the head of the Argus Academy, a former police officer, had once said to her. Not in class, but during a break—when he told her about a particularly dangerous situation in his former job. *If your gun has been taken from you, you are still left with the most superior weapon of all: the power of words.*

That had sounded more like a Zen master than an ex-cop. But at least it was a nice quote. Could it prove itself in practice?

Penny was not a skilled speaker, although certain people claimed she had a tongue like a sword. And that she often yapped too much. Pah.

"Wilhelm, please listen to me," she began hesitantly. She deliberately addressed him by his first name. *Building trust*, as it was called in criminal psychology. "You

are not a cold-blooded killer. You judged all those murderers Johanna exposed, didn't you? Justice is important
to you. You have the highest moral standards, and surely
you apply them to yourself, too!"

In the aforementioned TV crime shows, this appeal to
conscience sometimes worked magic. But what was it
like in real life?

Keep talking, Penny. Wilhelm seemed to be listening to
her. At least he was looking at her. Instead of firing his
pistol.

Trying not to let her tension show, she continued:
"Even if you get away with Johanna's murder—you won't
be able to live with this crime. Not in the long run.
Surely you've already realized that, haven't you? You
didn't kill just anyone, but the love of your life."

At these words, the old man lowered his gaze. He
blinked. Swallowed hard. Only the barrel of his gun did
not move a millimeter.

Penny continued to speak. Slowly and as poignantly as
she could: "Love is the most important thing in life. You
were the one who told me this. I'm sure you remember,
it was only a few days ago. Love—and family. Right? You
won't kill Miriam now too; I just know it. You love her
like the daughter you always wanted. You said that yourself, also."

Out of the corner of her eye, Penny noticed that tears
welled up in Miriam's eyes at these words. And that, as
if in slow motion, she lowered her revolver.

Oh my goodness!

But then Wilhelm reacted as well. Whether to Penny's

words or to Miriam's emotional outburst, only God knew. The only thing that mattered was that he also lowered his gun. Hesitantly, even more slowly than Miriam, but still.

Finally, his arms just hung limply, like a discarded doll's. A tortured sound escaped him, then the old man suddenly buckled at the knees—and went down.

His head slumped on his chest as if it had become too heavy to hold up any longer. And then, finally, Wilhelm let go of the gun. It slipped from his hand and came to rest on the floor beside him.

Cautiously, Penny took a step toward him.

He did not react. He was sobbing uncontrollably now and buried his face in his hands. He no longer seemed to notice what was happening around him.

Penny carefully put one foot in front of the other. She reached the spot where the gun lay, bent down for it, and picked it up. Done!

She quickly moved away a few steps and now pointed the Beretta at Wilhelm. But the man who had been murdering people for decades no longer seemed to pose any danger. He was only a desperate old guy who wept bitterly.

24

"Get up," Penny said, for the third time. "Let's get out of here!"

But Wilhelm Lindner took no notice of her. He was still crouching on the floor of the old cemetery cottage. His gaze was fixed on Miriam—and suddenly he began to talk again.

"I did it for Johanna," he said in a brittle voice. "Someone had to take care of that criminal scum she exposed, right? And you couldn't count on the police. They just didn't take your grandmother seriously!"

Miriam turned her head away. She was sitting on the lowest step of the musty staircase, and Jakub, who had finally unfrozen from his rigidity, was squatting next to her. Together they made a picture that would have stirred even a heart of stone. Agitated, frightened, paralyzed with shock.

"Do you think it was easy for me?" Wilhelm pleaded. He held out his hands to Miriam, but lowered them the very next moment.

"I am not a brutal, aggressive person, by God! But one does have social responsibility. Moral obligation! You can't just stand by and watch these murderers and criminals go unpunished. Already looking for their next victim!"

Miriam wiped the tears from the corners of her eyes,

but new ones immediately formed again.

"I did it for Johanna!" Wilhelm repeated in a desperate voice. "I wanted to be her hero! So that she didn't have to deal with these monsters. I would have done anything for her to make up for the mistake of my life. That I spurned her ... back when we were young and she loved me."

"Johanna would never have wanted you to become a murderer," said Penny. "No matter what the reason!"

He shook his head vigorously. "She didn't understand me, that's true. When she found out what I had done—for her!—that's when she turned her back on me."

"She had suspected you for some time, I think," Penny said. "As far back as the last couple of cases. And in her subconscious, maybe even much longer. She probably didn't want to see the truth at all because it was too horrible. The man she loved ... a mass murderer! Otherwise, she probably would have found out years ago, no matter how much she believed in divine justice. After all, she was a master of her craft."

She received no answer. Which didn't surprise her at all.

"Anyway," she continued. "Johanna recorded her suspicion in her latest diaries, didn't she? You had to assume that; you knew her habit of keeping records of her cases. Even if you never entered the archive yourself, during Johanna's lifetime. At the first opportunity that presented itself after her murder, you staged this break-in – to destroy the passages that could be dangerous to you. It was just stupid of you to leave the pages about Christiane Wittmann in place. By doing so, you confirmed her innocence instead of casting suspicion on her!"

Wilhelm ignored her.

He addressed Miriam again. He didn't seem to care about anything anymore—only that at least she understood him. "We had endless conversations, your grandmother and I. After she'd confronted me about the vigilante justice. She insisted I go to the police and turn myself in. She pushed me, more and more every day. But I hoped that she would come to her senses. I did away with this murderous scum for her sake! And I have done a service to society."

"You killed Johanna," Penny interjected. "You are no better than all the men and women you have judged!"

Wilhelm cried out in anguish, "I didn't want to kill her! I loved her! But she was waiting for me in my room, that night when I came home—"

"That night you killed Christiane Wittmann, didn't you? She was the latest victim of your mania for justice. You returned to the hotel after you had disposed of her body, I suppose. And Johanna confronted you. Her patience with you must have ended, now that you had committed another murder."

"Christiane was a cold-blooded poisoner! She killed her own husband. And her son-in-law! And she did not feel the slightest remorse for her actions. Yes, she even boasted about it when Johanna confronted her. Should I have let this witch marry the next unsuspecting man? Only to murder him as soon as he makes the slightest misstep?"

"How did you kill her?"

"I poisoned her, of course. An eye for an eye, a tooth for a tooth."

"And where did you bury the body?"

Wilhelm gave no answer to this question. "Johanna noticed the dirt on my shoes," he said instead. "When I came home that night. There was also some mud on my shirt, I had overlooked that. But she had known everything for a long time anyway. She told me to my face that I had killed Christiane. She called me a psychopath, a homicidal mass murderer, and she insisted that I turn myself in to the police that very night. We fought terribly. Finally, she ran out of the room, trying to get to the phone to call the police herself—" He broke off. His shoulders were trembling. He narrowed his eyes.

"You followed her," Penny said. "You caught up with her at the top of the stairs, didn't you? And then you gave her a push. It was murder. Own up to it."

"No, that's not true!" Wilhelm howled.

"And you killed Irmi, too," Penny continued, unperturbed.

Miriam jumped up from the stairs and pressed her hands against her ears.

"Stop it!" she cried; her voice dangerously close to hysteria. "Please! I can't take it anymore!"

The last few hours were just too much for her, Penny thought—and she couldn't blame her. She herself would have liked nothing better than to run screaming for the hills. But that was out of the question, of course.

Without taking her eyes off Wilhelm, who was still

kneeling on the floor, she went over to Miriam and put her arm around her shoulders. Her client, who was trembling all over, snuggled up to her for protection.

With her other hand, Penny still clutched Wilhelm's pistol. She did no longer expect him to come at her now, but she wasn't going to make the mistake of being careless again. At the slightest wrong move by the old man, she would pull the trigger. And hit her target—no matter what her instructor had said about her at weapons class. The safest place was not in front of her gun, but behind it, damn it!

She had to finish this, as much as she herself longed to finally hand Wilhelm over to the police and disappear under the covers of her bed for the next two weeks. First, get the full confession out of him and record it with her mini-microphone.

Who knows what he would deny later, once he had himself under control again.

"Why did you kill Irmi?" she addressed him again, while pressing Miriam's trembling body against her.

Wilhelm also looked exhausted, but he also seemed to want to bring the matter to an end. Was he still hoping that at least Miriam would understand him? Or did he just want to get his actions off his chest?

"She was standing there, at the foot of my bed," he said. "She snapped me out of my sleep with a movement or a noise she made. At first I really thought it was Johanna— who had come to haunt me. Of course, I don't believe in ghosts or similar nonsense. But I was half asleep and not in my right mind."

"And then?" Penny encouraged him.

"I begged her to forgive me. I swore to her that I hadn't wanted her to die. Then our eyes met—and I realized that it wasn't Johanna standing there in front of me at all. Although she wore the glasses I knew so well. The eyes, the look, they were wrong, even in the half-light. Maybe also the voice, although Irmi imitated it really well."

"How did you murder her?" Penny continued.

"I didn't!" Wilhelm protested. "It was an accident—as the police have already determined. I jumped out of bed when I realized that I wasn't looking at a ghost. That it wasn't Johanna haunting me in my dreams. That's when Irmi took flight. She ran out into the hallway, and I pursued her. She was a very athletic woman, and I am an old man. But still not so ancient that she could have shaken me off immediately. I stayed on her heels, she kept running, all the way into one of the disused side wings of the hotel. She must have realized that I was not going to be outpaced, so she turned into one of the old guest rooms, stormed out onto the balcony—and tried to climb down the gutter."

"Which came loose from its fixture in the process."

"Yes, exactly! It wasn't my fault. That old building is just terribly dilapidated. It was an accident!"

"How convenient for you," Penny said. "If you had caught up with Irmi before she crashed, I'm positive she wouldn't have survived it either. In fact, I'm sure of that. But an accident was much better, of course. No further trouble with the police for you."

25

Early the next morning, Penny and Miriam sat together in the breakfast room drinking coffee. Just the two of them.

For once, the young hotel manager wasn't scurrying around like a busy worker bee serving guests, but had an XL-sized steaming mug in front of her, warming her hands. Deep dark circles surrounded her eyes, but she still managed to give Penny a thin smile.

"I'm so grateful to you," she said, for what must have been the fifth time in the last half hour.

Penny could barely keep her eyes open. She hadn't gotten to sleep yet, and her hands and feet ached from the cold of the endless night that lay behind her. Or perhaps from the shock that was still in her limbs. The breakfast room seemed empty and deserted without the other guests. A real lost place.

They had turned Wilhelm over to the police, still in the cemetery. This time Penny had had no trouble getting the officers to go into action. She had called 112 and promised the officer on duty the confession of a murderer, confirmed by eyewitnesses and an audio recording. Within fifteen minutes, two police cars had shown up on the scene.

Wilhelm had not resisted his arrest. As he was being shoved into one of the police cars, he gave Miriam one last pleading look—which she did not return.

Penny went back to the hotel with Miriam and Jakub in the other police car, and they were immediately bombarded with some initial questions by the officers. They would probably have to make more detailed statements later today.

After the police left the hotel, Jakub disappeared into his room. Without a word. He was probably depressed because he had not been able to prove himself as the fearless detective and protector of women that he would have liked to be.

Theo hadn't shown up yet—which puzzled Penny. It seemed that Miriam had not called her fiancé, which would have been only natural after all the traumatic experiences of the night. Maybe the end of this relationship really was already in sight.

And Armin? He had also been conspicuous by his absence in the last few hours. Perhaps he was once again stalking around somewhere outside, because at night was the best time to photograph lost places, as he claimed. Or maybe he was still looking for the diamonds.

"How did you do it?" Miriam suddenly asked. "How did you figure out that either Jakub or Willi had to be Grandma's killer?" She was still clutching her coffee cup, but there was now a hint of curiosity in her eyes.

"Oh," Penny said. "I was in the dark for quite a while. It was all so confusing, even though there weren't that many suspects. It wasn't until I read your grandmother's diaries that I got on the right track. When I discovered that the murderers disappeared far too often, became fatally ill or had strange accidents, I realized that someone had taken justice into their own hands. Your grandmother herself, however, was rather out of the question. I didn't think it was compatible with the pious devotional pictures she pasted in the books. Besides ... well, committing murders yourself, for whatever reason, just doesn't fit a detective. I would never do something like that. Although, of course, I don't want to compare myself to your grandma. I'm nowhere near the professional she was."

She reached for her coffee cup and took a warming sip. "And also, there was the break-in at the archive. Those pages being torn from several notebooks. The pattern fit with repeated instances of vigilante killings. If it had been merely a single case in the past, the burglar who ravaged the diaries would have removed pages from only one volume. As Wilhelm has confirmed to us, your grandmother had been suspecting him for quite a while, and she probably recorded that in her journals."

"Until she caught him in the act of murdering Christiane Wittmann. Well, almost."

Penny agreed. Then she added, "I also came up with Wilhelm or Jakub as the prime suspects because an outsider wouldn't have been able to murder your grandma so easily. Johanna's mistake was that she probably just didn't believe her killer capable of harming her. Otherwise, she would have been on her guard."

Miriam just nodded her head.

"So, Armin was out of the question," Penny said. "Your grandmother didn't know him well enough."

And the suspicion that he wasn't after Miriam's affections, but something else entirely, had not been erased from Johanna's diary. Which Armin undoubtedly would have done if he had been the burglar. Penny, however, left this clue unmentioned to Miriam.

"I'm sure Johanna wouldn't have turned her back on your Theo so imprudently either," she continued instead. "I don't think she liked him very much. Besides, he had an alibi for the break-in, since he was out with you on the night in question."

More wordless nodding from Miriam.

"Irmi would have been my prime suspect as far as vigilante justice was concerned, I must confess. She had a, well, let's say, very biblical view of justice. But then –"

"– she was murdered herself," Miriam added somberly.

"Right. That left Christiane Wittmann. We already knew that she was capable of murder—but she wasn't the one who broke into the hotel and tore the pages out of the diaries. She would hardly have left the passages intact that concerned herself, of all things. Those pages where Johanna accused her of murder. But why had she disappeared without paying her bill? On the day your grandmother died, of all days? Of course, that looked suspiciously like a new case of vigilante justice when it finally dawned on me that we were dealing with it. That left only Jakub and Wilhelm ... and you."

"Me?" asked Miriam in amazement.

Penny grinned apologetically. "In principle, yes. You should never make the mistake of ruling out a suspect until you have solid evidence of his innocence. Even if they seem harmless. But you probably wouldn't have torn the pages out of the diaries to cover your tracks, while at the same time pointing out to me that your grandmother would never have trashed a book that way. Besides, you hired me to investigate the murder case, after all."

"So, Willi and Jakub were the only two left," Miriam said.

Penny nodded. "Wilhelm was in love with your grandmother. Jakub was a longtime loyal employee. I don't think she would have believed either of them capable to murder her. Hence, I started my little experiment with the two of them."

"*Your little experiment*? You could have gotten yourself killed, Penny!"

Penny shrugged, though she secretly had to agree with Miriam.

"It all turned out well, after all!" she said lightly. "But I have to admit that I would have put my money on Jakub rather than Wilhelm. Your janitor also has the kind of sense of justice needed to become a vigilante, I think. Though he's not as extreme in his views as Irmi had been. My mistake was that I never asked Wilhelm about his attitude in this regard. But he probably wouldn't have said anything radical so as not to give himself away."

"I still can't believe he killed Grandma," Miriam said in

a strained voice.

"It's hard for me, too. He really did love your grandmother. But where there is great love, there is also potential for great disappointment. The fact that she didn't understand why he was acting as a judge must have hit him hard. He wanted to be a hero to her, and she saw nothing but a murderer."

They were both silent for a few minutes. Miriam sipped her coffee while Penny grabbed a croissant from the bread basket and spread it with butter and apricot jam.

"By the way, I don't think you're as unlike your grandmother as you think," she said then. "It was very brave of you to follow me to the cemetery. Completely crazy, but also very courageous!"

Miriam smiled wryly, and Penny bit into the golden-brown croissant. She must have eaten thousands of these sinful delicacies in her life, but this one tasted better than any had before.

26

"There's one more thing," Penny announced after only crumbs remained of the croissant. "I have some very good news for you. Regarding your inheritance."

Miriam raised her eyebrows. "Seriously?"

Penny nodded. "I know now where your grandmother hid the diamonds. I came up with the solution when you showed up last night, with her revolver in your hand."

"The revolver? I don't understand ... What does it have to do with it?"

"Nothing at all. It was your trembling hands that gave me the solution."

Miriam looked at her uncomprehendingly.

"Believe it or not, the diamonds have been right under your nose all these years. Since your 14th birthday, I'd say, if I got the timeline correct."

"I don't understand a word," Miriam protested.

Penny grinned. "Remember your grandmother's strange wording in the letter she left you? *Learn from the past, and you'll never be a beggar again.*"

"Yeah, sure, but –"

Penny reached for her hand. This morning, Miriam was again wearing the bracelet with the colorful stones, beads, and childlike animal charms.

"What do you call this kind of jewelry?" Penny asked her.

"Huh? I don't know."

"The standard term is charm bracelet, I believe. But a more old-fashioned word, especially here in Austria, is *beggar bracelet*. Never heard of it?"

"Oh, yeah, I guess I have."

"*Learn from the past and you will never be a beggar again*. That was a hidden clue from your grandmother about this bracelet! She was really saying: Read my diaries, which tell you about my past and how I became the detective you could be one day. Discover the flame symbols next to those passages that concern you, and remember where you've seen them before. Find David Blüthenstein's letter, and then you'll realize that the beggar bracelet isn't a beggar bracelet at all. Admittedly, the last part was a little tricky."

"I only got the part about the flames," Miriam said meekly. "But that was it."

"Exactly. You recognized the symbols. And that's how we discovered the letter from David Blüthenstein. In which he bequeathed your grandmother some particularly beautiful gems from his estate."

"But we didn't find them because the envelope was empty."

"It was empty, Miriam, because your grandmother gave you the contents as a gift long ago. In the form of that beggar bracelet you got from her. Which is anything but a beggar's bracelet."

Miriam was still looking at her in confusion. The poor thing was really slow on the uptake this morning.

Penny brushed her fingertip over one of the colored

glass stones hanging from the bracelet.

"That, my dear Miriam, is a colored diamond. Five of them dangle from your bracelet, if I've counted correctly. One red, two blue, one yellow, and this huge pink one here, which I'm sure is worth half a million euros by itself. For all five taken together, we're easily looking at a million euros, I'm sure. My mother's crazy about bling like that," she added. "So I know a little bit about gem prices."

Miriam gasped for air. She stared in disbelief at the bracelet she'd been wearing for half her grown-up life.

"Of course, without David Blüthenstein's letter and your grandma's clue, I'd have thought myself that these stones were worthless glass," Penny added. "As would probably everyone else who sets eyes on that bracelet. Including you. The settings of the stones, the actual chain and the rest of the charms are indeed cheap stuff. Silver at best, by the looks of it. And plastic beads to boot. The perfect camouflage."

Miriam took off the bracelet and looked at the diamonds with wide eyes. Once again, her hands trembled. But this time at least with joy and excitement, instead of fear.

"Your grandmother was pretty crazy, if I may say so," Penny continued. "I mean, with that scavenger hunt she came up with for you, she risked you never finding your inheritance!"

Miriam grinned. "Oh, that's sooo typical for Grandma. She was all about riddles, while she never cared about money. Or even about jewels. She probably didn't even have a clue about the true value of those gems. How could she have known that this guy David Blüthenstein had left her such a fortune!"

Penny shook her head with a laugh. "I'm sticking with it: completely crazy!"

Miriam joined in her laughter—and stroked the bracelet tenderly.

"Grandmother must have thought I would eventually solve her riddle," she said after a little while. "She really wanted me to carry on her life's work, to be a sleuth like her. She thought I had a talent for it, but in this one instance she was wrong. Completely wrong. But maybe I would have at least read her journals at some point, who knows. Anyway, she could be sure that even without the diamonds I wouldn't starve. The hotel covers my living expenses. And I like it here. I'm not missing anything. Grandma knew that."

"So you're going to stay here?" asked Penny. "Even though you're a wealthy woman now?"

"Most definitely. I love this old house. Maybe I'll sell one of the diamonds and tackle some repairs sometime. I could also invest a little in marketing, what do you think? Maybe we should make a name for ourselves as a *lost place*, with a wider audience. That's pretty trendy right now, isn't it?"

Miriam was beaming. The new possibilities that had opened up for her with the diamonds seemed to fire her imagination.

"These are great ideas," Penny said—and spontaneously hugged her client. That wasn't in the detective training manual, but to hell with it! You had to be allowed to be unprofessional once in a while!

"One more thing," she added. "If you want to keep Armin Keyser as a paying guest for a while longer, you shouldn't tell him about the bracelet. I'm afraid it's the search for the diamonds that's keeping him here at the hotel. Not you."

"Oh," Miriam said—and reflexively brought one of her fingers to her lips to nibble on the nail.

But then, to Penny's surprise, she lowered her hand again. "Grandma warned me about Armin once, just before she died. She said he wasn't the right man for me; that's all she told me. But I have to admit I didn't want to hear that."

"You know," Penny said. "Your grandmother was a very good judge of character."

"Well, not so good after all. She hadn't realized for ages that Willi was a murderer!"

"Love is blind," Penny said—and in the next moment felt pretty silly for spouting such wisdom.

Miriam frowned. "Things haven't been going so well between Theo and me lately," she confessed spontaneously.

Penny nodded. "That's the impression I got, too. Just wait a bit longer maybe before planning your wedding?"

"I will."

This time it was Miriam who hugged Penny. She squeezed her tightly. When she let go again, she said, "I want you to take one of the diamonds. As your fee. You're the best detective in the world!"

"Out of the question," Penny protested. "Didn't you listen to me about what these things are worth?"

"Yes, I did," said Miriam, "and you're not getting the pink one. I've taken quite a liking to that one myself. I think I'm a little like your mom in that way." She grinned broadly and her eyes sparkled. Then she let the bracelet slip through her fingers again. "You told me you're in detective training right now. So you're still at the very beginning of your career. I'm sure you could use some start-up money."

She scrutinized the diamonds on the bracelet, among all the plastic beads and silver pendants.

"You get this blue one here," she decided. "It's particularly shiny, I think."

Enjoyed the book?

Please consider leaving a star rating or a short review on Amazon. Thank you!

More from Penny Küfer?

DEEP DIVE INTO DEATH
Penny Küfer investigates, Book 3

Axel Sandorf, business magnate and visionary, has achieved what others only dared to dream of: he is cruising the oceans aboard the largest private submarine yacht the world has ever seen.
Penny can't believe her luck when she, of all people receives an invitation from the elusive billionaire. It's supposed to be a pleasure cruise under the sea—but where Penny goes, the first murder attempt is not long in coming. Instead of exotic fish, the ambitious young detective is soon chasing a poisoner who seems to outsmart her in every way ...

About the author

Alex Wagner lives with her husband near Vienna, Austria. From her writing chair she has a view of an old castle ruin, which helps her to dream up the most devious murder plots.

Alex writes murder mysteries set in the most beautiful locations of Europe and in popular holiday spots. If you love to read Agatha Christie and other authors from the "Golden Age" of mystery fiction, you will enjoy her stories.

You can learn more about her and her books on the internet and on Facebook:

www.alexwagner.at
www.facebook.com/AlexWagnerMysteryWriter

Printed in Great Britain
by Amazon

84791223R00112